It Happened at Percé Rock

Melanie Robertson-King

King Park Press

Published by King Park Press
Copyright © Melanie Robertson-King, 2021
Percé Rock Image: Graham Hobster, Pixabay
Couple on Beach: Shutterstock, Inc.
(Signed model release on file with Shutterstock, Inc.)

It Happened at Percé Rock is a work of fiction. Names,
characters, places and incidents are the product of the author's
imagination or are used fictitiously. Any resemblance to actual
events, locales or persons, living or dead, is purely
coincidental.

ISBN: 978-1-990371-00-4

DEDICATION

For Joan, my friend and number one cheerleader.

ACKNOWLEDGMENTS

Thanks to everyone who put up with my daft questions during the research of this novel. Without your help, the book would not have come to fruition.

I'd like to thank Joss Landry who reminded me how amazing the sunsets and moonrises are in the village of Percé.

Huge thanks to my beta readers Patricia Capitain, Suzy Turner and Nancy Chapman.

If I've missed anyone by name, I apologize.

Special thanks to my husband, Don, who continues to support and encourage me, and provides a shoulder to cry on when things don't go well. He redesigned my website making it mobile-friendly and taken charge on the domestic front giving me time to write.

One

Melissa and Iain's condo, Water Street, Saint John, New Brunswick

Melissa Scott raced along Water Street carrying the bed-in-a-bag she purchased from *jonathans*. The cranberry and navy tartan quilt, bedskirt, and pillow shams were perfect to grace the bed she and Iain would share after their wedding.

The narrow cords on the bulky paper shopping bag cut into her fingers, forcing her to switch it from one hand to the other as she walked.

An enormous ship was docked at the Marco Polo Cruise Terminal near the city's Port Authority, across the street from her future home. Once she moved in with Iain, this would be an everyday view. Diamond Jubilee's terminus was also on this side of the Saint John River but closer to the Bay of Fundy.

Her fiancé worked as a guard at the Saint John Regional Correctional Centre on Old Black River Road and was scheduled to be on duty. She planned to take the purchase to the condo on her lunch break so that after work, she could go straight home and take her black and tan dachshund for a walk. The breeder registered him as Frankfurt's Champion Beauregard. Melissa found that way too stuffy. From the time she got him, she always called him Buddy or Bud for short.

The condominium would be empty, so there was no need to stick around. Melissa would drop the package inside the door and go back to the store. When she reached the top step, she pulled the key from her purse, unlocked the deadbolt and leaned in to sit the parcel down. All appeared fine until she started to leave. A noise upstairs made her freeze. She tried to rationalize the sound. The wind had picked up since she left *jonathans*. Most of her journey was spent brushing her hair out of her face, so the breeze billowing the curtains could have knocked something off the nightstand. She pushed the leaded-glass door open wider.

One of Iain's steel-toed boots lay in the centre of the foyer, the other near the steps as if he had kicked them off in a hurry. A pair of women's heels were close by. Articles of clothing littered the hall floor and stairs to the upper level, most noticeably his uniform shirt. If he was at work, why was it there? Any other time she dropped packages off, their future home was immaculate. Things didn't add up. Tiptoeing up the wrought iron-railed oak staircase, she nudged a white t-shirt, another piece of his clothing, aside with her foot.

On the landing, grunting and moaning emanated from the master bedroom. Melissa crept to the door, reached for the handle but pulled her hand back. Did she want to discover the cause of the noises? She sucked in a deep breath and swallowed, then turned the knob and flung the door open.

Iain's bare back and broad shoulders filled the gap — slender feminine legs encircled his waist. He lay in what would become their marital bed with someone else.

"I-I-I," she stammered, unable to form the words. A strangled moan formed within her and intensified in volume.

He immediately froze then leapt out of bed, pulling on his uniform trousers. The woman he was having sex with snatched the sheet and pulled it up to her chin to cover her nakedness.

Melissa turned and darted down the stairs.

Iain followed her, tugging up the zipper as he charged out

of the bedroom. "Mel, wait." At the front door, he grabbed her by her upper arms and spun her around. "It's not what you think."

"Looks perfectly clear to me what was going on in our bed."

"It's not *our* bed — yet. If not for your stubbornness and prim and proper ideals, we'd be sharing that bed now. Paying rent and utilities on one place instead of two."

"Not so long ago, you were willing to go along with my decision. You knew I wanted our wedding night to be the first time we made love, and you agreed."

He let go of her and threw up his hands. "That's still over six months away. You expect me to wait that long? No one does that anymore."

"I do." She twisted the engagement ring on her finger and worked it past her knuckle.

"No, Mel. Please don't do that."

"Give me one good reason why I shouldn't."

"I love you." He knelt on one knee in front of her and held her hands. Tears blurred his vision. He had made an enormous mistake. One that would haunt him forever.

"Get up. You're making fools of both of us."

When he stood, Iain gripped Melissa's upper arms again and kissed her hard on the lips.

She pushed him away from her. "You couldn't be faithful to me before we're married. What makes you think you can be afterwards?" Melissa drew back her right arm. Seconds later, the tinkle of the platinum band on ceramic tile echoed throughout the room.

With the door handle gripped tightly, she turned to leave.

"No, Mel, please. I'm sorry. I swear it will never happen again," he pleaded.

"Too bad. Tell it to her upstairs." She fled, leaving the door wide open behind her.

Iain retrieved the engagement ring then dropped on the second step from the bottom. The diamond lost its sparkle. At that moment, it was dull and lifeless like his and Melissa's relationship. He blew it — huge. The tears he fought to contain escaped. The one person in his life he truly loved, and he hurt her in the worst possible way. Never would she believe a word that came out of his mouth again. If only he hadn't let his hormones rule his brain. He loved Melissa.

A long, slender, bare leg brushed against him, and his mistress sat beside him in silence. Her head rested on his upper arm, but he didn't have the energy to object. The biggest mistake he made in his life was getting involved with Yvonne Carruthers, the warden's wife.

The woman was roughly ten years his senior, but appearance-wise looked to be younger than him. She had fascinated him since he first met her, mainly because she was so different from her husband. She was tall, slim, blonde-haired and blue-eyed. Her spouse was pot-bellied, short and bald, granting credence to the phrase 'opposites attract.' Slowly, she wore Iain down with her suggestive winks and seductive smiles. Then there was her clothing. Short skirts, stiletto heels, and low-cut tops. What red-blooded male wouldn't find that interesting?

Yvonne never set foot inside the institution, at least not when Iain worked. She always remained in the parking lot, which was an excellent idea given her sexy appearance. Some days the woman leaned against the side of her silver Mercedes.

On other days, she waited in the driver's seat for Iain to approach. She opened the car door, eased around, and held her hand out for assistance. He fell for her every move. Damn his weakness. He should have resisted her come-ons. Her flirting. He didn't, and now he had lost the one woman in the world who made him whole — Melissa Scott.

A sigh escaped that seemed to come from his toes. Yvonne reached out, took his hand and led him back up the stairs to the bedroom. Mesmerized, he followed. After what he did to Melissa, he would never win her back, so he might as well let his hormones have their way.

Melissa darted down the front steps. Gulping back sobs, she ran back to the store and straight to the women's washroom. Tears streamed down her cheeks. She wiped them away with the back of her hand, but her vision remained blurred. How could Iain cheat on her? They were solid. At least she thought so. He never gave any indication before he was unhappy. How long had he and this woman been involved? Not that it mattered. He lied. She would never forgive him for that.

Once inside one of the cubicles, she locked the door. Melissa sat on the toilet and buried her face in her hands. Within seconds, the gut-wrenching cries she'd struggled to contain on her run from the condo escaped. She pulled her cellphone from her purse.

The wallpaper displayed a picture of her and Iain at Irving Nature Park. She quickly went through the settings and chose a generic image to replace it. The last thing she wanted was his face filling the display every time she used her phone. She saved other photos of him on the device, but now was not the time to scroll through and delete them. Instead, she opened the messaging app, scrolled to Danielle Fortin's name, switched to the emojis screen, and tapped a string of broken hearts.

Silently, she willed the woman to reply.

Melissa and Danielle had been friends for as long as she could remember. They grew up in the same neighbourhood in Ottawa and attended the same schools. When Melissa left home for the Maritimes, Danny stayed behind. Her sense of adventure lay in the village of Percé on the Gaspé Peninsula.

When they were both younger, Melissa went with the Fortins to their cottage that overlooked Percé Rock. They walked over the causeway to the rock when the tide was out, much to the nesting gannets' chagrin. The memory made Melissa wish she were that age again and vacationing with the Fortin family.

By the time he reached the top of the stairs, Iain's conscience had gotten to him. "I think you better go, Yvonne."

"You weren't thinking like that before our interruption."

"I never expected Mel to walk in on us. This was to be between us — our secret. A one-off, never to repeat."

"Yet it has. Today wasn't the first time we were intimate. I like a bit of fun as much as the next person, but you should have told me you had a girlfriend," she said with her hands resting on her hips.

The pose pulled the shirt tight and tested any feelings of remorse to their limit. Iain had to beg Melissa to forgive him. He loved her, not Yvonne. She was just sex, although he doubted his fiancée would see it that way.

While he thought of ways to apologize, no grovel, to Melissa and plead with her to give him another chance, Yvonne gathered her clothes and began to dress.

He picked up his phone. Unable to find the words verbally, he tapped out a message.

I'm sorry. I love U. I never meant 2 hurt U. Pls give me another chance. A crying face emoji followed.

Would she even respond? He hoped so. He said some hateful things in the course of the conversation, which he wanted to take back, in addition to his dalliances with Yvonne Carruthers.

The phone vibrated in her hand — one new text message. Iain's name topped the list flagged as unread. She couldn't bear to read it, nor delete it. Every conversation they had would be gone if she deleted it. No matter how much she hated him at the moment, she couldn't do that. For now, she chose to ignore it.

Another vibration. This time it was Danielle.

OMG! What's wrong?

Melissa tapped out a response.

Caught Iain with another woman. In our future marital bed.

She paused, hit delete and removed the second sentence. Danielle was smart enough to understand the drift of things with the broken hearts previously sent.

Are you sure you didn't get the wrong end of things?

Nope. Deleting it didn't work. She had to spell it out.

Iain's cheating. Caught him red-handed.

There was no sugar coating, and she couldn't make it any more straightforward if she tried.

So sorry, sweetie. You don't deserve that.

Melissa needed to get away from Saint John; the sooner, the better. She couldn't go back home to Ottawa, although she needed her mother more than anything at the moment. Her siblings all had lives of their own. They didn't need her landing on their doorsteps with her dirty laundry.

Sucking in a deep breath, she dropped her phone back in her purse and stood. She had to get back to work. As it was, she was already late.

When she leaned on the sink, her long, brown hair tumbled forward. She reached up with both hands and tucked the tresses behind her ears before splashing cold water on her face and fixing her makeup with a wet paper towel. The raccoon mask from her mascara and eyeliner, while still there, was no longer as noticeable. Now it resembled dark circles from not sleeping well. The ladies' washroom was near the elevator, so Melissa could get up to the floor, housing the offices unseen, with any luck.

With the way her lunch break unravelled, the last place she wanted to be was at work. Would the store manager, Walter Peters, let her take the afternoon off? How did she ask? It's not like she was ill.

She stepped out through the open doors and straight into the path of the man. "Slow down, young lady."

"S-sorry," she faltered and bolted towards her desk, the back of her hand covering her face. Melissa may not have been sick before, but she was now. Almost taking out her boss didn't help. She collapsed in her chair and laid her head in her arms, and wept.

It was apparent Melissa wasn't going to answer his text message. Iain didn't blame her because his actions gave dirty, rotten scoundrels a good name. He was the worst possible scum.

Yvonne tucked her blouse inside her short skirt. She

smiled at him. The same smile that turned him to jelly in the beginning. The one that caused all the trouble. Not the smile; it was his weakness.

He stood stalk still until she picked up her bag and started for the landing. She placed her hand on the back of his head and whispered in his ear, "You know where I am."

Her hot, moist breath weakened his knees. There he went again, succumbing to this woman's charm. He had to resist, but she made it impossible. Her long fingernails traced seductively down his neck, his back. Yvonne tested his resolve to its limit.

"If Mel won't take me back, maybe, but I'm going to try to win her affections again, and if I succeed, there won't be any you and me. If I don't, we'll see." Why on earth did he say that last bit? The words asked for trouble. Iain turned and walked away.

A short time later, the front door closed. Iain exhaled. Until that moment, he didn't realize he had been holding his breath. He pulled Melissa's engagement ring out of his pocket and brushed the diamond against his pant leg. The move didn't bring back the missing sheen. Only winning her back would do that.

He shuffled about the condo, gathering his clothes. To return home for his rendezvous with Yvonne, he feigned illness at work. Not expected back, he had the rest of the day to find Melissa and apologize and attempt to make things right between them — again.

White t-shirt tugged on, he trotted down the stairs to put on his shoes. Once done, he headed to the inside entrance to the complex's garage area.

His red, older model Honda Civic occupied the corner bay. Over the years since he bought it as a beater, he worked on it — bodywork, a spoiler, new rims, and low-profile tires. The finish had oxidized, but with an aftermarket product and a lot of effort, Iain brought the paintwork back to its original lustre.

The car's engine had been finely tuned, and now when he stepped on the accelerator, the car had power. During the process, Melissa teased him about spending more time with his car than he did her. She was right. He barely spent any time with her. Between working at the correctional facility and restoring his 'baby,' not many moments remained to spend with her.

The new warden arrived in February of the previous year. Once the last of the snow finally melted, Yvonne appeared with her silver Mercedes. That was a ride you didn't take out in a New Brunswick winter.

Iain started the Honda and backed out of the parking space. The automatic garage door rose as he approached, and he sped out, squealing the tires on the concrete.

jonathans was a short drive up Water Street, but there was no place where he could wait for Melissa to leave work. A few spots were between the condo and the pub, but they were too far back to see the store's entrance. Beyond the store, another parking area lined the side of the road. Iain pulled his Honda into a vacant stall and turned off the ignition. He would wait all afternoon if that's what it took to see and speak to her.

Angled into the corner of the building, the doors were invisible from this vantage point. The rear-view mirror offered little help, and in no time, he had a kink in his neck from craning to survey the entrance.

Iain stretched before walking to the front and raising the hood. Under the pretence of inspecting the engine, he leaned on the passenger side fender and stole glances down the street. If Melissa walked up the hill on Princess Street when she left work for the day, he would never see her. If she came by here on her way to King, it would be the perfect spot to wait — and he'd persuade her to take him back.

"Problem?"

Iain cocked his head in the direction of the voice. A Saint John police cruiser had pulled adjacent to his car.

"Not now," he answered. There never was an issue with the motor, but he had to say something.

"Good, because you can't fix it here. I'll follow you to make sure everything is all right."

The city's finest thwarted his best-laid plans. He dropped

the hood, eased in behind the wheel, and turned the key. The car sprang to life. Now to find a place to go not too far from *jonathans* so he could return to his waiting game. Where could he go?

Iain pulled away from the curb. At Union Street, he made a right. So did the cruiser. At the junction where the liquor store was, he went left then entered the parking lot. In case the cop waited nearby, Iain got out of the car and pretended to head into the shop.

On the way, he stole a glance to the right. The police car had moved on. Iain turned around and returned to his vehicle. Here, he was near Melissa's apartment. Maybe closer to her house would be better. He would be less conspicuous in a residential area. Passersby would think he was waiting for someone. He was, just not in the way they would assume.

A right turn onto Wellington Row, and he headed towards the church at the end of the block. Another right here, followed by a left and Iain, found himself on Melissa's narrow street where parking was prohibited on both sides. Instead, he turned down the one next to her building, made a U-turn, and parked in a no-parking zone near the corner. No way he would miss her if she came this way.

As each vehicle drove past, Iain peered in the windows on the off-chance Mel caught a ride home with a co-worker. What if she was already home? Then his efforts would be for nothing. Best wait and watch a bit longer; if she didn't pass by, either in a car or on foot, then he would check her apartment. The corridor and stairway were a common open area so he could get all the way to her door.

There she was. A small, white hatchback slowed, with Melissa in the passenger seat staring out the window. Iain waited for them to pass, then jumped out of his Honda. He couldn't be too eager, yet he couldn't waste the opportunity to speak with her.

When the building's door creaked shut, he walked around the corner. The car was unoccupied, which meant whoever brought Melissa home was in the apartment with her. Now, he would have to wait even longer to beg her to take him back and swear to her it was over and would never happen again.

The person wouldn't stay long. Coburg Street was narrow, and you couldn't park on either side. However, a green sign bearing a white P opposite the converted Victorian led to confusion since one indicating no parking was directly above it.

After what seemed like hours, a car door closed, and an engine started. Iain returned to the intersection as the car disappeared behind the house on the curve. He trotted up the steps and slipped in through the front door. Melissa's apartment was on the top floor of the house. Taking the stairs two at a time, Iain worked his way to her door. When he knocked, Buddy started barking. The scratching of toenails scrabbling on the laminate flooring grew louder until the small dog was on the opposite side.

The door opened a crack. Melissa's tear-streaked face filled the narrow gap. "Iain. I don't want to see you — ever," she cried.

Not taking her seriously, he pushed his way into the apartment. "We need to talk. You don't know how sorry I am."

Melissa backed away and folded her arms. "For what? For what you and that woman were doing or getting caught?" Defiance filled her voice.

Iain threw his hands up. "What do you think?"

"You don't want to know my answer."

He grabbed her wrists.

"Let me go," she seethed.

"Not until you listen to me."

Melissa wriggled beneath his grip. "Do you want me to call the cops? How do you think that would go with your job? If you want to become unemployed, keep it up. If not, leave."

She was right. His position at the correctional facility would be gone if the police arrested him. He let go of her and slinked towards the door.

Two

Melissa's apartment, Coburg Street, Saint John,
New Brunswick

Melissa sighed when the apartment door slammed shut behind Iain. Her world crumbled a few short hours ago. The man she planned on marrying — had bought a condominium with him soon after their engagement — was a lying cheat. At least she found out now before the wedding.

Her hand trembled when she tried to put the chain's end through the hasp. She didn't usually worry about it because not many people came up to her apartment, except those she expected. Until today, the peephole and lock were adequate. From now on, the deadbolt would be engaged and the chain secured. Time would tell if Iain took heed of her threat to go to the police. No matter how much she hated him at the moment, she couldn't ruin his career.

Melissa flopped on the sofa and curled up in a ball. Her tears flowed again. Buddy joined her, wriggled his way under her arm, and pressed against her. His gesture offered some comfort, and Melissa stroked his sleek coat. His soft ears felt like velvet beneath her fingers.

Iain parked his car in front of the pub across the road from Melissa's work. Hardly the ideal location to see her but better than when he was farther up the street beyond the store's entrance.

Today, he didn't have the time to linger. He needed Mel to arrive in the next five minutes, or he would miss her. So far, she made it abundantly clear she wanted nothing more to do with him. He had to persuade her otherwise.

His tryst with Yvonne was a mistake, and while he enjoyed their sexcapades, it was Melissa he wanted to be making love with.

His cellphone vibrated in his pocket, and Iain plucked it out and gazed at the screen. Yvonne's name filled the display. What did that woman want now? She was not giving up. He swiped his finger over the glass.

As long as we carry on as before, Ed will never find out, but if you dump me, I'll be straight off to tell him every sordid detail.

Did the woman have no shame? Blackmail? Now what? No matter how much he wanted to make it up to Melissa and win her back, he couldn't take the chance. Should Warden Carruthers find out about the affair, he would be unemployed in a blink of an eye.

The phone vibrated again — another message from Yvonne.

I'm serious, Iain. I always get what I want, and I want you.

How to reply to this text. He required delicacy to not anger the woman and send her raging to her husband about his employee, who she had been screwing regularly.

Never the best typist, he struggled to tap out a message. Auto-correct didn't help either. Its suggestions weren't the words he intended.

I need time. Things 2 work out. Condo 2 list. Owe Mel her portion of the downpayment. C what she wants 2 do with the stuff she bought 4 the place.

After he hit send, Iain sighed and flopped his head back

against the headrest. She might back off and give him some space if she thought they wouldn't have a place to meet. A decent idea, but she was demanding, so the chances of it actually happening were slim.

He needed to speak with Melissa. What he had to say was best said face-to-face — not sent in a text.

Melissa unclipped Buddy's leash and trudged up the steps to her apartment. The last flight winded her every time she climbed them. Despite his short legs, the little dog had no issues at all. He ran to the head of the stairs and stared down at her.

Pet-friendly apartments were hard to come by, and she was lucky to find this one, which was also well within her budget. Another plus was she could walk to and from work in less than fifteen minutes unless she had to stop for supplies or the weather was foul.

Her phone vibrated when she reached the upper landing. Likely, just Iain making a nuisance of himself again. He didn't deserve a response. His recent behaviour spooked her, and she asked the police to have a word with him. Iain spent hours sitting in his car outside the store or across from her home. At least this time, he wasn't watching and waiting. Maybe threatening to obtain a restraining order worked. She hoped so.

After opening her door, Buddy charged through the gap and up the ramp to the sofa. Days like this, she wished she had his energy.

Melissa kicked off her shoes and sat her iPhone on the island, which also doubled as her table. The sun beamed in the windows. Early morning, and by now, it was warm. She pulled down the shades and drew the curtains. Yes, it made the apartment dark, but the baking hot rays wouldn't heat up the place.

When she started to repeat the process in her room, Iain's red Honda sat on the other side of the street. Out of habit, she consulted the calendar she kept on the small dresser in the corner of the bedroom. He should be at work today. On the early shift. Why was he outside her apartment? Perhaps the restraining order threat hadn't worked. So far, she only threatened to get one. It could cost him his job if she went through with it.

She snatched up her laptop and returned to the kitchen. Her phone vibrated again. Worried it might be Iain, Melissa hesitated before opening the protective case. The display showed two new messages. She tapped the icon on the screen and sighed with relief when neither was from him. Both were from her friend, Danielle.

You OK?

That message was followed by a longer one.

Last-minute cancellation here. Why don't you come? Do you good to put some distance between you and Saint John.

Summers spent at Fortin's cottage as a youngster were always so much fun, despite Danielle's older brother teasing them. Sometimes his friend, Paul Sutton, came along, too. A trip to Percé, even if just for a few days, would give her a reprieve from Iain.

Let me see if Mr. Peters will give me the time off. I'll let you know. Have to check train and bus connections, too.

Forty-five minutes from now, she had to head out the door to her job in the accounting department. She could use the time to search the transportation schedules. No, best to leave that until she knew for sure if her boss would let her take time off. Given the recent events, Melissa didn't think there would be any problems. The man was a kind-hearted soul.

She cracked open a window to allow fresh air into the apartment. Iain's car no longer sat next to the curb. He either gave up or waited by *jonathans* and would accost her there or left for work. So long as he was not anywhere near her, that's all Melissa cared about.

Danielle fist-pumped and yelled when Melissa's reply came through. 'Yes,' drawing out the last letter, so she sounded like a snake hissing. Now to put part two of her plan into action.

She needed her brother and Paul to be at the cottage, too, and neither one had to know match-making was on her agenda. Getting away from Saint John and her cheating boyfriend, Iain, would do Melissa a world of good, but her friend didn't need to know she was being set up with another guy. If Melissa caught wind of that, she'd stay home.

Her phone pinged again, putting a stop to her ideas.

When do you want me?

In times like this, Danielle wished Melissa owned a car. If she did, leaving early in the morning, she would be in Percé by supper time. It took about eight hours driving, depending on the number of breaks you took. Instead, she had to rely on the trains and or buses.

Danielle looked up her brother's name in the contact list on her phone.

Booking cancelled. Have the place to myself for a couple of weeks. Why don't you & Paul join me? Be like old times.

She hit send and waited. The message appeared benign. Nothing untoward that would arouse suspicion. If Gilles suspected she was up to something, he wouldn't be receptive to the idea. Like Melissa, would the guys be able to drop everything on short notice to spend some time at their family's summer home?

Her smartphone vibrated in her hand.

When?

Basically, the same question Melissa asked.

Next week too soon?

She held her phone to her chest, hoping things would work out.

Let me c if I can juggle some things and get back 2 U.

Three

Construction site, Ottawa, Ontario

No sooner had Gilles hit send than the possibility his sister was up to something niggled at him. Danielle had a massive crush on Paul when they were all kids. Did she still? He was confident Paul felt the same way about her, too, and would explain why she asked him to come along for a holiday. Oh well, if they both still shared feelings about each other, it would be their problem to deal with, not his.

He returned to the construction trailer and removed his hard hat. Summer was a busy time on the building site. Would his boss let him take a couple of weeks off? The firm employed another foreman, so he wouldn't be leaving them in a lurch.

Gilles dropped into the swivel chair behind the desk. Stacks of invoices and blueprints buried the computer keyboard, so he moved them aside. He pecked out an email to his employer with two fingers asking for the following two weeks as vacation time. Gilles assured the man the project was on schedule — a bit ahead, actually — and reminded him another person capable of stepping in during his absence worked for the company. Now he played the waiting game.

He pulled out his phone while he waited and searched for

Paul's contact information. Did he text him now or after he heard back? If he waited too long, his friend might've made other plans for the time.

Danny wants us 2 come 2 the cottage in Percé 4 2 weeks starting next week. What do u think? Waiting 2 hear from the boss if he lets me take time off 2 go.

He'd have less time to think about whether or not his request would be approved if he kept busy.

Mr. Peters was most understanding and granted Melissa the leave she so badly needed and assured her that her job would be waiting when she was ready to return.

These days, Iain stalked her less frequently than before. She had not made contact with him. On the occasions he called out to her, Melissa picked up her pace and ignored him. Her actions must have worked, and the fact she no longer wanted anything to do with him sunk in at last.

She took her laptop to the kitchen island and scoured the transportation schedules. The train didn't go the entire distance to the village where Danielle lived. It only ran between Moncton and Campbellton, but that did nothing for either end of her journey. A trip to the place she spent so many enjoyable summers and where she needed respite from the city, work, and her ex.

No matter how she worked it out, she would be spending the better part of nine hours overnight in a station. At least the final leg departed from the same location as she arrived at. Was it worth the expense? Would her dog be allowed, or would she need to board him at a local kennel? She read the websites for the transit services and found the information she sought. Buddy had to ride in a carrier, but he could travel with her. That reduced her worries.

"Appears like we're going on an adventure, Bud."

The black and tan dachshund lifted his head from his soft bed and laid it back down, not concerned or interested.

Credit card extracted from her wallet, she booked her passage. Once she completed that job, she contacted Danielle.

All good. Leaving on the 4th and will see you sometime on the 5th.

Transportation sorted, next on the to-do list was laundry and pack for herself and Buddy.

The crate was in the sizeable hall closet, along with a washer and dryer. The last time she used the cage was six months ago to take Buddy to the vet for his annual check-up. The pungent aroma of wet canine greeted her when she picked up her pet's container, so she removed the towel and tossed it in the washing machine.

The bus to Moncton didn't leave until eleven o'clock, and the station was a short distance from Melissa's apartment. She could let Buddy walk that far and put him into his carrier for the two-hour ride before boarding.

The scenery along the four-lane highway was boring, so Melissa pulled out her Kindle. At least the bus had Wi-fi so she could entertain herself online or delve into the latest crime book she purchased. She couldn't bring herself to read a romance novel or even a chick-lit one.

When the coach arrived in Moncton, Melissa had a four and a quarter-hour layover before the train to Campbellton.

Shortly before the boarding call for the train, she took Buddy outside once more.

Her backpack, stuffed to capacity, hung over the overhead bin. One of the railway employees suggested she stow her bag and the pet carrier in the luggage racks at the end of the car, but she refused. No way would she leave her dog alone back there with people tossing their suitcases in the compartment haphazardly with no regard for bags already in place.

Buddy's cage filled the floor space, forcing her to put her feet on top of it. Far from comfortable, but if someone had a ticket for the seat next to her, she would be forced to ride this way the entire trip.

Four hours later, the train slowed for the approach to the

Campbellton station. When Melissa stood to pick up the dog's crate and pull her backpack down, her legs cramped. The awkward position took a heavier toll on her than she expected. Once she moved along the aisle to the exit, the cramping subsided, and the sensation returned to her extremities.

The station's concourse was conspicuously empty despite the train's arrival and the number of people who exited from the platform area with her. Some of the other passengers had people there to meet them. Couples embraced, making Melissa's pain from her breakup with Iain rush back. She blinked back tears and dashed to the nearest exit.

At least here, there was a twenty-four-hour Tim Hortons within a short walk of the terminal. Before striking out in its direction, Melissa returned Buddy to his cage. She came back to the station with a medium coffee with two cream and two sugars, known in Canada as a double-double, and a fruit explosion muffin, which she shared with her dog.

Once they finished their snack, Mel lay down on one of the benches, using her backpack as a pillow. It was uncomfortable, but she made do. She tucked the animal carrier partway under the seat with the door facing out. Her hand dangled in front of it. That way, the dachshund could see her and not be scared.

Melissa had set the alarm on her smartphone the previous night before settling down. She didn't want to sleep in and miss the connecting bus for her journey's final leg. It took her a moment to realize what the sound was that roused her when it went off.

The bench was not the most comfortable place to spend seven hours. Still, with her late arrival and early departure, in addition to lack of funds, it made no sense to pay for a hotel room. Soon she would be at the Fortin's cottage with her friend, Danielle.

When the driver pulled the vehicle into the parking spot opposite Percé's Tourist Information office, Melissa grabbed Buddy's carrier and bounded down the steps. The iconic pierced rock couldn't be seen from here, blocked by the bluff and red-roofed, white houses. Her destination was the one atop the hill. She clipped the lead to the dachshund's collar, and they began their walk.

How long had it been since her last visit to the Fortin home here in the small Québec town? It had to be before she went to university in Saint John. Two years there on the business course, and more before that. Those summers in Percé were so much fun. This trip was a first for Melissa. The first since Danny took over running the guesthouse started by Mrs. Fortin when the couple retired to their cottage year-round. It was on their way back to Percé from Ottawa that a head-on collision took their lives.

The tang of the brackish water and scent of dried seaweed competed with cooking aromas from the various eateries throughout the village. Melissa picked up her pace once she turned on to Rue Mont Joli. Sure she and Danielle texted, face-timed, and had video chats, but it was nothing like being together. After making the ninety-degree turn, the walk became a steep ascent. Two days in cramped seating didn't do her legs any favours, and as she strode up the grade, her calves burned.

Soon the obélisque, once attached to Percé Rock, appeared, as did the outermost section of the iconic piece of the landscape just off to the right of the bluff slightly below the cottage's level.

This trip was exactly what Melissa needed. Away from Saint John. Away from Iain and away from the pain. The house near the crest of the hill was not here the last time Melissa visited. A white picket fence poked out from the overgrown wild rose bushes on her right. The spicy aroma of the blooms filled the air. She was almost at the driveway.

Gravel tire tracks with a grassy hump between led upwards. She didn't remember hills like this before. But then, they always came in the car. Still, they went down to the beach and walked out to the rock at low tide.

Now they were on the Fortin property, Melissa unclipped Buddy's leash, and he ran ahead of her as fast as his short legs could carry him. Occasionally, he stopped and looked back.

Carrying the loaded backpack and animal carrier, the combined weight grew heavier with each step.

A curtain twitched in the window. A screen door slammed shut. Danielle appeared around the corner of the building and rushed towards her. Buddy jumped straight up and down on his back feet, begging for attention. At that moment, Danny only had eyes for Melissa.

Two arms wrapped around Melissa and hugged her warmly. "It's wonderful to see you," Danielle gushed.

Melissa pulled back then embraced her friend again, all the while trying to stem the tears that threatened to flow.

"How was your trip?" Before she could answer, Danielle continued. "Long, I suppose and spending the night in the station must have been just awful. Come on in, and we'll get you settled. Then if you want, you can take a shower or a hot bath. Up to you."

"Would love that. I feel pretty grungy."

An unfamiliar pick-up truck sat next to a BMW in the parking area in front of the guesthouse. "I thought you said you had a cancellation."

"There are plenty of rooms here. Besides, I have a surprise for you."

Oh, Lord. Danielle's surprises were usually monumental. What did the girl have for her this time?

The decor in the living room had changed since Melissa's last visit. Gone were the fishing nets with shells stuck in them from the walls — now painted a pale sky blue and accented by paintings. The well-worn cottage furnishings had also been replaced. Now, comfortable overstuffed sofas and armchairs in cyan and yellow stripes formed a seating nook near the fireplace. White coffee and end tables completed the look.

The kitchen and dining area opened up off this redecorated space. Instead of tiny, boxy rooms, the entire section of the downstairs was now open concept. What a difference it made. It must have cost a small fortune for Danielle to make all these changes.

"I'll show you and your little dog to your room, and you can meet us in the kitchen once you've had a chance to freshen yourself up."

Meet us? Who's us? Melissa shook her head and followed her friend to the room she had been assigned. "This was your parents' room. Are you sure about me staying in it with Buddy?"

"Yes, silly. If not, I wouldn't have put you in it." Danielle pushed the door open.

As bright and cheery as the front room was, this one was completely opposite. Antique dressers and chests of drawers lined the cream-coloured upper walls. Wainscotting topped with a chair rail, the same shade as the hard furnishings, covered the lower portion. An enormous iron-framed bed sat at an angle in the corner. The bed coverings were deep burgundy.

"I couldn't bear to part with mum and dad's furniture, but I tried to make my mark on the room. The ensuite is through here." She opened another door.

The walls were bright white subway tile from the floor to the ceiling. A neo-angle shower took up one section of the room, and a free-standing soaker tub stood in front of the frosted window. A massive chocolate brown vanity with a clear vessel sink was next to the door, and the toilet hid behind the open door.

Back in the day, there was no ensuite. It was another small bedroom only accessible through the room she entered. "Is business doing well?" Surely, it couldn't have been making enough income to make changes on this scale.

"It's all right. Steady. Dead in the winter. No one wants to come to the ocean in those months."

"But … these renos must have cost you a fortune."

"There was money from the estate. And it helps to have a brother in construction." Danielle smiled. "I only had to pay for the fixtures and materials. Gilles did the rest."

"I forgot he went into the trades."

"I'll leave you to get freshened up now." Danielle backed out of the room and closed the door as she left.

Melissa heaved the backpack from her back, and it landed on the ceramic tile ensuite floor with a thud. She rooted through it to find her cosmetics bag and other toiletries. A tray of shampoo, conditioner, bath and shower gel sat on a shelf by the bathtub. She picked up one of the containers. These were high-end products, not the cheap ones her budget allowed and she brought with her.

After turning on the taps, she squirted a generous dollop from one of the squeeze bottles into the tub, creating a layer of foam on the water. Buddy snoozed on the mat next to the soaker forcing Melissa to step over him to climb in.

Refreshed after the luxurious soak, Melissa wrapped a thick white bath sheet around her. This bathroom was something she could grow accustomed to. It certainly put the dinky one in her apartment to shame.

Dressed and a bit of makeup applied, Melissa left the room to meet Danielle and whoever 'us' was in the kitchen. Her heart leapt into her throat when she saw Paul Sutton standing at the island. She had such a massive crush on him as a teenager and would be mortified if he knew.

A head poked up above the open refrigerator door. Gilles, Danielle's brother, was there. All right, what was her friend planning?

"Thought with what you just went through with Iain, it would be fun for us to get together like old times," Danielle said.

"Danny told us about your break up. Really sorry, Mel. You didn't deserve that." Paul placed his hand on her shoulder.

Heat rushed to her cheeks. If her face was as hot as it felt, she was beet red.

"Wasn't sure what time you'd arrive, so I didn't plan anything fancy for supper tonight. I'm defrosting some ground beef and buns, so we're having burgers. I still make them the way Mom did."

A faraway look crossed Danielle's eyes. Melissa could relate, sort of. She hadn't lost her mother but her father. Being the youngest, she was the apple of her dad's eye — his little sunshine.

"At least let me help," said Mel.

"When it's time. In the meantime, why don't we go sit on the verandah and catch up." She pulled a pitcher of iced tea from the fridge and put it on a tray with four glasses. "You bring this out, bro? Thanks."

Danielle wrapped her arm around Melissa's shoulders, and they headed for the porch.

A square glass-topped table surrounded by chairs stood at the far end. Melissa chose the chair against the wall, which afforded the best view of Percé Rock. Buddy huffed, then dropped to the rug under the furniture at her feet.

"I hope I've timed it right for the tides. I want to walk out to the rock like we used to as kids."

"Not only that, but the full moon is in the next day or so. Fingers crossed we have clear skies."

Gilles and Paul finally joined them. Danielle poured out four tumblers of iced tea and handed them around.

"Mel wants to go to the rock. Let's all go. It will be like the good old days."

"No, Danny. I'd rather go on my own. I need some alone time — even here. Especially here."

"But ..." she objected.

"Let her be, sis. She knows her own mind."

Danielle's expression showed her disappointment.

"At least let me make the first trip by myself. Maybe we can go as a group another time," Melissa offered, hoping to appease her friend.

A smile formed on Danielle's face. Crisis averted. The four sat around the table talking, laughing and reminiscing about the days they came as children for two weeks every summer. Mr. and Mrs. Fortin had the patience of saints, putting up with their childhood nonsense. Melissa still had a jar of rocks collected from the beach over the years. Maybe she'd start a new collection on this trip. Start afresh, just like she was doing in real life.

Would Iain have wanted to come to Percé with her? He wasn't much of a traveller. So much so, they never discussed a destination for a honeymoon. Getting him to agree to the wedding in Ottawa was hard enough. Why did his name pop

25

into her head? She was with friends hundreds of miles from him and Saint John and the scene of his betrayal.

When it came time to start the hamburgers, Melissa pulled an enormous bowl of ground beef out of the fridge. "Are you planning on feeding an army, Danielle? You have enough meat here for one. And not a small one either."

"Now there's an idea. A bunch of handsome soldiers — they would take your mind off things." A broad smile formed, and her eyes sparkled. "I'm making lasagna tomorrow night, so I got it all out today."

Melissa sighed, relieved she was no longer the object of her friend's matchmaking. With both women working on preparing the meat, it took no time for the patties to be seasoned to perfection and formed, ready to go on the grill.

After a delicious meal and more laughs, Mel took Buddy out for one last bathroom break and headed straight to her bed. The trip's length and lack of a decent night's sleep in the station had taken their toll on her.

Four

Fortin's Guesthouse, Percé, Québec

The sun rose from behind Percé Rock, leaving it in silhouette; the enormous orange orb reflecting on the rippling water of the Gulf of St. Lawrence. At the base of the cliff, waves lapped on the pebbled beach. The sound soothed Melissa.

For a summer morning, it was chilly — damp more than anything from the overnight dew. She shivered and pulled the crocheted afghan around her shoulders. Melissa spent most of the night tossing and turning and, after many sleepless hours, gave up and went outside so as not to disturb anyone.

After her long trip and one night in the station at Campbellton, she figured she would sleep like a newborn the first night in a comfortable, warm bed, but it was not the case. Dreams of Iain's betrayal tormented her. Melissa knew it would take time to get over him, but she hadn't banked on replaying the scene when she caught him and his mistress repeatedly at night. If she were still in Saint John, she could understand the nightmares, but not here in Percé at her friend's family cottage, far from where the incident took place.

Buddy stirred on the porch beside her chair. She patted her

27

knee and invited him to her lap, and cuddled him close. He wouldn't betray her. They were a team — an inseparable team.

The two would walk along the beach and over the causeway to explore Percé Rock more closely if the tide cooperated later that day.

The screen door creaked, and Melissa turned in its direction. Paul stood in front of it in a pair of plaid flannel sleep pants and his bathrobe open, exposing his bare chest. He held a cup of coffee in his hand.

"Penny for them."

"They're not worth it," she replied.

He handed her the steaming mug of dark roast. "You take mine. I'll go make another. You look like you need it more than I do."

Melissa smiled. The heat rose to her cheeks because, as a young girl, she had a massive crush on Paul Sutton. If he noticed she did, he never let on but would have had to be blind not to see how she followed him. Even now, his chiselled features and hazel eyes sent a shiver down her spine.

Then everything changed. He and Gilles graduated high school before she and Danielle did. Paul won an athletic scholarship to Harvard and left in September of that year, and she had not seen him since. Gilles skipped post-secondary education and went into the trades. She moved to Saint John, Danielle stayed in the Ottawa area.

About eight-thirty, pots and pans clanging from inside the cottage rang out. Paul still sat on the verandah with Melissa. They barely spoke from the time he joined her. Nevertheless, having him there, not asking awkward questions or passing judgement, comforted her.

Was it her fault Iain looked elsewhere for his physical needs? He didn't want to wait for their wedding night to make love for the first time but went along with her wishes.

Same with her not moving into the condo before they became man and wife. Melissa was miffed at him for doing so straight away, but he gave up his apartment as soon as they received word the deal had gone through and knew the closing date. He had a point that it made no sense to pay rent on two apartments and a mortgage on their future home.

Danielle stuck her head out the door and said, "Breakfast is ready, you two."

Paul grabbed Melissa's empty mug and waited for her to stand before letting her precede him inside. When she walked past her friend, she was confident the girl winked in Paul's direction. Danny was playing matchmaker.

Over a delicious meal of bacon, eggs and home fries, Gilles spoke. "You've got an excellent day for the tides. Not a lot of wind, sun. Tide is already out."

"Thanks," Melissa said and reached for another strip of crispy bacon.

"Not sure how long you plan on being down there, but you should be back on the mainland by one at the very latest. Wouldn't want to see you stranded."

"I'm not stupid, thank you very much."

Gilles shook his head. "Not what I meant." He ripped his slice of toast in two and shoved one of the pieces in his mouth.

"I heard on the radio earlier this morning, thunderstorms are forecast for later today. Make sure you keep an eye on the sky as well as the tide," said Danielle.

"You must recall the fire and brimstone ones we got when we came here as kids," said Paul.

Melissa nodded.

"Do you remember the way from here?" asked Danielle.

"Yup. Right out the driveway to where the road ends, then down the hill to the sandbar."

"You're wrong. No way down from the top. Only takes you to the viewing platform. You need to hang a left when you reach the public washrooms and cut across to Rue Blard. Go right to the end, and you'll find the stairs to the beach," said Gilles. "Or you can go back to the highway and head right towards the Percé Rock Hotel. The street you want is just before it. Mind you, it's faster to go the first way I mentioned."

Unable to believe she forgot how to go from the cottage to the shore, Melissa excused herself and returned to her room to prepare for her adventure.

Dressed in a pair of cut-off jean shorts, a white blouse, and her Birkenstock sandals, Melissa started down the driveway. Not yet off the guesthouse property, she had to roll up her shirtsleeves because she was so warm. Buddy trotted along in the grass bordering the lane beside her.

She crossed to the other side to face the oncoming traffic and strode down the hill. Other cottages, cabins and B&Bs lined the narrow road. How Danielle managed to eke out a living running her establishment with so much competition around amazed her.

The entire village was practically nothing but hotels, motels and other tourist accommodations. Melissa preferred the Fortin home that now operated as a guesthouse under her friend's management. Competition was a good thing, right? Plenty of that abounded in Percé. What about in winter? Most of the businesses likely closed for the off-season.

The breeze soughed through the meadow next to the roadside, bringing with it the flowery scent of the wild roses and Black-eyed Susans. A lawnmower droned in the distance, and the fragrance of fresh-cut grass wafted over the air. These pleasant smells overpowered the faint tang of the brackish water. Percé Rock towered over a red-roofed white house farther up the road. A host of other white buildings, some with red roofs, some with other coloured shingles, dotted the otherwise gold and green landscape.

In the distance stood a substantial green-roofed, white building. Between it and Melissa, a gravel path went off to the left. It must be the one Gilles spoke of. The wheelchair-accessible public bathrooms nestled at the base of the grade, and a crushed stone track opened up beyond it. They weren't here the last time she came to Fortin's Guesthouse. How many years ago was that?

Melissa set out down the gravel roadway, which didn't appear to go anywhere. Did Gilles pull a prank on her? A joker to the end, he often played tricks on her and Danielle when they were children. This could be another one of his jokes.

A gust of wind stirred up the fine particles of sand in the parking lot. Melissa turned away, but still, grit ended up in her eyes when she crested the hill. She blinked a few times to try to flush it out but couldn't make her eyes water enough to eliminate the pesky grains. An enormous building stood in the centre of the cleared area. Cars lined the sides of the structure, but there was empty space on this side. About five minutes later, she came out at the hotel Gilles mentioned. He didn't lead her astray.

The closer to the water she got, the more excited Melissa became, reliving a memorable time in her childhood. It was a rite of passage to hike from the mainland to Percé Rock. The only ones who didn't take part in this pastime were the locals. Likely at some point in their lives, they, too, made the trek.

At the set of wooden stairs leading to the shoreline, Melissa picked up Buddy and descended. It was a short walk from here to the shoal, where she would cross. Once she reached the bottom, she put the dog back down, and the pair struck out.

Water lapped over the edges of the causeway and pooled in the lower sections of the sandbar. Melissa lifted her dachsie before stepping from the drier beach towards the mammoth chunk of shale and limestone. A lump formed in her throat as she stood gaping at its near-vertical cliff faces.

With Buddy tucked under her arm, she picked her way across. Unsure if it was due to the time of day, the time of year, or the bad weather forecast, there were not many people wandering around. No one strolled along Rue Mont Joli either. Strange.

Because he was well behaved and came when called, Melissa had no qualms about unclipping Buddy's leash and putting him down. At first, he stayed by her side, sniffing the ground or raising his nose to catch a whiff of something. The scent of rotten eggs wafted through the air, no doubt brought on by rotting seaweed, occasionally overpowering the more pleasant aromas.

Melissa made herself comfortable on a boulder and pulled

out her phone while Buddy amused himself. She had no new messages. Not hearing from Iain was a blessing. Maybe he realized they were finished.

She took pictures of the village from this vantage point and Buddy playing on the sand and pebbled shore. She was far too close to the rock to photograph it. She would have to wait for another time. The quay where the tour boats left from would be the best location. Melissa snapped a couple of selfies with Percé looming behind her — some smiling, some with pouty lips before returning the device to her back shorts pocket.

Loud barking and growling jolted her from her reverie as Buddy antagonized a company of gannets. Squawking seagulls soared overhead. One landed nearby and stared at Melissa with its beady yellow eyes. It took a few steps closer, ruffled its feathers and stepped back again. Living and working near the water in Saint John, she was used to seeing them. This one was different. It was more intimidating, almost like it was daring her to move so it could attack, like in the movie *The Birds*.

Water splashed by her feet. The tide was coming in. She wasn't here that long, was she? Pulling her phone out, she checked the time. Yes, she had been. She had to act and fast or be cut off. "Come on, Bud, it's time to go," she called to her dachshund, but the animal continued harassing the waterfowl. She lunged for him, and he darted away closer to the arch — the most dangerous place of all here.

A clap of thunder rumbled in the distance. Things were quickly becoming dire. Melissa had to get her dog and return to the mainland before the thunderstorm hit. Too late. The skies blackened, and the rains pelted down. Lightning streaked across the sky, followed by yet another crash. How close was the storm? If she counted between the flash and the thunder, the longer the gap, the further away the inclement weather was. There was more to the calculation, but at this point, it made no difference.

Strong winds pushed the incoming tide and created whitecaps. Huge waves churned and crashed over the sandbar cutting the two off from the shore, making it difficult to stay upright. Melissa finally lassoed Buddy, and she sheltered close to the opening. Danielle would send Gilles and Paul to find her if she was late returning to the cottage.

Gareth Young raked his fingers through his dark hair as he walked towards the end of the pier. This time in Percé was supposed to be therapeutic for him. If anything, it was the exact opposite. He still woke in cold sweats, his breathing laboured as the horrors of war returned. For some unexplained reason, as time went on, things got worse instead of better.

His aching right arm throbbed, indicating an imminent change in the weather. He took shrapnel from his shoulder to his hand when a roadside bomb exploded nearby during his tour of Afghanistan's Panjwayi District. The surgeons said he was lucky. He still had the body part and the use of it and his hand. They told him the scars would fade in time. The physical ones had, but not the ones inside.

Gareth lifted his arm as high as he could before the pain prevented him from raising it higher. He dropped the wounded limb to his side and rubbed the painful joint to ease the discomfort. It didn't work. He had enough pins, screws and plates attached to the bones in his injured extremity to open a hardware store.

When the intense ache became unbearable when he had times like this, he wondered if he would have been better off having the bloody thing amputated. At least then, he wouldn't be in constant misery. While he recovered in a German hospital, others who had undergone amputations still felt their missing limbs. Phantom pain, they called it.

The other escape from his chronic discomfort was suicide. Extreme, but his agony would be over. He couldn't do that to his parents — leave them thinking he took the coward's way out. One of his specialists had suggested he get a motorcycle, but not one of those crotch rocket things. The vibrations from the bike would help his painful shoulder.

A lot of research and a fair chunk of money later, Gareth bought a classic Norton 850 Commando Hi-rider. He had checked into Harleys but couldn't afford one. The motorbike he purchased was used but had been well maintained.

It looked brand new. He was happy with his purchase and had ridden it from the military base at Valcartier, where the Van Doos were headquartered to here on a ride around the Gaspé. Over the days, he had to stop numerous times because of fatigue to rest his arm. He found when he was riding, the shoulder pain was hardly noticeable.

Dark clouds formed overhead, and the wind picked up. A few raindrops splattered on the ground then became more steady.

The sound of a powerful marine engine grew louder. One of the whale-watching tour boats appeared from behind the stack on the outer edge of Percé Rock. It was one of the Zodiacs. Something else caught Gareth's eye. A flash of white near the arch of the megalith. He trained his vision on the location. Someone was stranded. The combination of the incoming tide and the storm cut them off from the mainland.

He waved frantically and pointed to where he saw the movement, but it was for naught. The Zodiac continued to the quayside.

As people disembarked, Gareth rushed over. "Someone's trapped out there at the rock. We've got to help them."

"Who would be stupid enough to be there in this?"

By now, the rain was a torrential downpour. Gareth's soggy shirt stuck to his skin. Before the pilot had a chance to refuse, Gareth leapt into the craft. "Come on, let's go," he coaxed.

"Cast us off then."

The men untied the vessel — one from the bow, the other from the stern.

On their way to the rock, a thunderclap that started out like the report of machine-gun fire took Gareth straight back to Afghanistan. His neck hairs prickled, and he covered his ears, squeezed his eyes closed, and dropped low in the boat. Loud noises were his nemesis, whether it was a car backfiring, thunder, construction blasting or fireworks. *Pull yourself together, man,* he urged silently. In this state, he was of no use to anyone, and it would take two people to rescue the stranded person.

He gulped in a few deep breaths then raked his fingers through his hair, his hand pausing at the hairline.

Eventually, he pulled himself into one of the seats facing the wheelhouse. Unable to make eye contact with the pilot, his eyes darted back and forth.

"You okay, man?"

Gareth nodded. What else could he do? Tell the guy his sorry tale from the war and how he suffers from PTSD? No way. That was private.

The boat approached Percé Rock, and the man in control cut back the engine. The bow sank into the water while the stern rose. Level.

"Can you get closer?" Gareth asked.

The man piloting the vessel maneuvered nearer, but far enough away he could keep the bottom from running aground despite the waves threatening to beach the craft.

Gareth leapt into the now waist-high water. The current pushed him off balance, and he stumbled. He reached out and grabbed Melissa's hand and gamely worked his way to her. Once he was close enough, he scooped her and the dachshund into his arms and waded back through the churning water to the Zodiac.

After dropping the two in the boat, he hurled himself over the side and laid on his back staring at the sky.

"What in the name of … were you thinking? You dummy, you could have drowned," the pilot scolded.

She met his admonishment with gut-wrenching sobs.

"I-I'm sorry."

"So you should be. If there's any damage to my boat, my livelihood, you'll be hearing from me."

"Don't be so hard on her." Gareth sat up. "Gareth Young, former soldier — still in the military — and knight in shining armour. And you're?"

"Melissa Scott, and this is Buddy."

He reached out to pet Buddy, and the dachshund snapped at him.

"Ungrateful little Wienerschnitzel."

"He's scared." Melissa defended her dog.

When they arrived at the quay, an ambulance waited; its lights flashing.

Five

Fortin's Guesthouse, Percé, Québec

Gilles glanced out the workshop door when the storm's cacophony was audible over the power tools' sounds. Where or when did it blow in? The sun shone, and the sky was cloudless when he went to fix the broken chairs for his sister.

A brilliant flash of lightning, followed closely by a deafening crack of thunder, plunged the room into darkened silence — a hydro failure. The question was, for how long? As children, he and Danielle watched the storms from the safety of a bedroom. Most often, in his, because she was afraid.

He leaned against the doorframe. Rain lashed through the opening and forced him to close the double barn doors. The light levels were too dim to work, even with hand tools, so Gilles decided to stop working for today and try again the next. Hopefully, by then, the electricity would be restored.

Sawdust covered his clothes, so he wiped his palms on his pants, brushed most of the crud off before he removed his shirt and gave the garment a vigorous shake. Danielle would flip if he dragged his dirt and grime into the house.

The rain let up, and he took advantage of the moment. Once he had the door closed and padlocked, Gilles sprinted across the yard to the verandah. Under the shelter of the roof, he turned his back to the house. The skies to the west were brightening. Soon the storm would be gone.

Red and white lights on a bright yellow ambulance flashed from the quayside. The back doors were open. Gilles turned and went inside.

"No further," Danielle ordered. "You're filthy."

Paul, standing on the far side of the kitchen island, raised his head. "Sure is quite the thunderstorm."

The hydro was on in the house. Only the workshop had been cut. The generator. His mother insisted they connect one not long after opening their home as a guesthouse. If she had guests, she had to feed them and clean for and after them.

"Mel not back yet?"

"No. I'm worried. She should've been back ages ago. Long before this storm blew in," said Danielle.

"There's an ambulance down at the quay. You don't suppose …"

Danielle scrambled into the back of Paul's BMW. Her brother rode shotgun. At least the back of Gilles' clothes weren't too dirty. If Paul minded, he kept quiet.

In less than five minutes, they pulled up behind the emergency vehicle.

A gasp escaped from Danielle's lips. "Holy moly, it's Melissa. Get out, bro'. I can't until you do."

Barely giving Gilles a chance, Danielle started pushing on the seat back and flipping the lever to release the catch. She stumbled when she exited but remained on her feet.

Melissa shivered on the steps in the rear of the EMS vehicle with a blanket draped over her shoulders. Her sopping, long brown hair stuck to her head while some clung to her cheek. Next to her sat a thirty-something guy who was also drenched, holding a similar covering.

"What happened?" Danielle rushed to hug her friend. A soft growl came from under the blanket. She pulled back one side of the cover. "Hey, Bud. Did you and your momma have some excitement?" She squatted in front of the dog and its owner.

Through chattering teeth, Melissa began. "I-I got c-caught out in the s-s-storm. B-B-Buddy was chasing b-b-birds and w-w-wouldn't listen to m-me."

Danielle squeezed between Melissa and the doorframe of the ambulance and put a motherly arm around her. "So then what?"

"G-Gareth, here ... h-he ..."

At that point, Gareth took over. "I persuaded the Zodiac pilot to take me out to the rock to rescue her. I'd been wandering the beach and was on the quay when I saw her. She was in danger. The whale watching tour was coming back, and we went out together."

One of the paramedics returned and checked Melissa's vitals.

"Can we take her home now?"

"Where's home?"

"Up there." Danielle pointed to the house on the top of the hill. "I'll make sure she's well cared for. See she's warmed up and into dry clothes."

"She really should go to the hospital or at the very least the CLSC to be checked out."

"I-I'll be fine. I-I just want to go home."

"Gareth, since you rescued our friend, why don't you join us for dinner?"

"You sure?"

"I wouldn't have asked otherwise."

"Thanks. I'll head to my hotel, clean up and be there. How do I get to your place from where I'm staying?"

"Where's that?"

"Motel Impérial."

"All right, so you come back this way like you're coming to the quay, but keep going to Rue Mont Joli. Turn on it and continue until you see the sign on your right, 'Fortin's Guesthouse.' We're up at the end of the gravel driveway. White cottage with a red roof and wraparound porch. You'll know you're at the proper place because my brother's skanky rust bucket of a pickup truck is there and our friend's BMW."

Gareth nodded with each leg of the journey as if committing the route to memory. His actions said he was not a local but a tourist who happened to be there at the right time.

"That car there." He referred to the sleek black beemer.

"That's the one."

"Any time in particular?"

"Soon as you're ready. Danielle turned to the paramedic. "What about your blankets?"

"Keep them for now. You can drop them at the Firehall when you're finished with them."

Danielle bundled Melissa into the back of Paul's car. "Can we give you a lift to your hotel?"

"Nah, you're alright. Tad crowded in there."

Gareth followed the BMW with his eyes as the car turned around and made a right turn at the intersection with the highway. Despite the paramedic's insistence, he and Melissa keep the blankets, he handed his back. With the afternoon sun beating down on the wool, he was too hot. On the walk from here back to his hotel, he would dry out.

The scent of the air was different now. There was a technical term for the phenomenon, but it escaped him. It was as though all the pollutants had been washed away, leaving only the fresh, clean fragrance of nature behind.

Why did he accept the invitation so readily? Before his Afghanistan tour, he would have considered doing so, but these days when he didn't know who he would be, he tended to isolate himself. Still, when he saw Melissa in danger, he had to rescue her. It was the honourable thing to do. Between his upbringing and his military training, if you could help someone, you did, had been drilled into his head.

He couldn't back out now. He said yes. Inside his motel room, he kicked off his soggy footwear, peeled his wet clothes off, and stepped into the shower. With the water turned as hot as he could bear, he stood under the spray and let it permeate his body.

When he was sufficiently warmed, he grabbed the towel. Gareth rubbed himself down before wrapping the terrycloth sheet around his waist. His duffel bag sat on the bamboo shelf in the closet. He swung the rucksack on the bed and took out clean clothes.

He had no other shoes with him. The only pair he brought were the black steel-toed boots that he wore into the Gulf of St. Lawrence. Now they squished with every step. He dug in his holdall some more and came up with sandals. They would do, which also meant he would have to walk. No way was he riding the Norton in flimsy footwear; that was asking for trouble.

Showered and wearing clean, dry clothes, he felt much better. Almost to where he happily anticipated being with people instead of holed up on his own.

Wet shirt and jeans draped over the shower bar, socks on the side of the tub, and black boots beside the sink, he was ready to go. As he picked up his wallet, Gareth changed his mind. The billfold was soaked, as were the contents. That would be a job for later. He left it lying open on the desk.

He jogged out the door, rolling up his sleeves as he went.

"You don't need to run me a bath. I'm quite capable of doing it myself," Melissa protested.

"After what you've been through today, you deserve some pampering." Danielle swept by her and headed straight to the soaker tub.

Melissa shook her head. Why did she agree to come here? The trip turned into a nightmare — first the episode at the rock, which was her fault because she let Buddy go off-leash. Huge mistake. Now Danielle fussed over her like an old mother hen. While she appreciated the gesture, Mel wanted to be on her own. The trip's idea was to spend some girlie time with her friend and try to get over her cheating ex-fiancé.

"Here you go. I put some Cypress bath salts in the water. They work wonders when you're chilled." Danielle grabbed the cozy microfibre bathrobe, and the enormous towel off the clothes hook on the door. "I'll pop these in the dryer, so they will be warm when you're ready for them."

When she disappeared, closing the door behind her, Melissa breathed a sigh of relief. She was alone, which is what she wanted.

She climbed into the tub and sank beneath the surface. The floral-like scent of the salts Danielle used wafted on the steam. What would she wear? Gareth didn't see her at her best. Hair pasted to her head. Blouse stuck to her skin.

It would take days for her Birkenstocks to dry. She brought a dress and strappy high-heeled sandals in case the girls went out for dinner one night, but that was over the top for a meal at the guesthouse. Melissa lay there and puzzled longer. Danielle returned with the warmed towel and housecoat when she yanked the chain on the plug with her toe.

Wrapped in the heated clothing, Melissa heaved her stuffed backpack on the bed. She had hung her royal blue lace, v-neck fit and flare dress in the wardrobe to allow the wrinkles to fall out when she unpacked after her arrival.

She pulled out a pair of black skinny jeans. So far, so good. Her white high-top Converse sneakers came out next. This was easier than she expected until she had to decide on a top — any colour but white. Yesterday, Danielle said supper tonight was lasagna and garlic bread. Out came her red-smocked camisole. Now to find a lightweight sweater for over it.

Rummaging more, Melissa discovered her black long open cardigan. She laid out the outfit and stood back. Too much? Not enough? Why did she care what she looked like for Gareth? She only met him a few hours ago. As it was, when she agreed to the visit, Melissa didn't know Paul and Danny's brother, Gilles, were going to be there. Maybe she was trying to impress Paul? She'd had a massive crush on him growing up. So had Danielle.

Dressed, hair dried, and makeup applied, she left the comfort of her room to meet the others.

When Melissa entered the open-plan kitchen, dining and living room area, Paul turned towards her and whistled. Heat rushed to her cheeks in a blush that, in all likelihood, matched the colour of her camisole.

Gareth hadn't arrived yet, so it was just the four of them. Not knowing if he had a vehicle or how fast he walked, although he wasted no time when he raced to her and plucked her out of the water and into the boat, it could be some time.

Going from memory, walking from where he said he was staying was likely about half an hour, but the last time she was here, she was just a kid, so what did she know? Besides, maybe the man owned a car and would drive up to the house? She assumed he would walk because she didn't own one.

"I'm glad you're all right," Paul said and wrapped her in a hug.

If she wasn't blushing before, she sure was now. Dumbstruck and cotton-mouthed, she couldn't speak to say thank you. All she could do was nod.

The room was warm, but was it that temperature or her own that caused the flush? Flames flickered in the gas fireplace, indicating the source of the heat. Buddy lifted his head from the blanket he commandeered from the bottom of his carrier and thumped his tail on the floor.

Danielle took Melissa's hand and led her friend to one of the armchairs in the seating nook. "Sit here where you'll be warm. Your hands are like ice," she said.

Would the mothering ever stop?

Soon after Melissa settled into the soft, overstuffed chair, a knock sounded from the screen door. She stood and turned, only to receive the evil eye from Danielle and sat back down.

"Come on in, Gareth," Danielle said, opening the front door and extending her arm in invitation. "Take a seat over with Melissa. You guys need to warm up."

Melissa rose again, smiled at Gareth and rolled her eyes at

her friend.

"Wow, you scrub up well," he said, then waited for her to sit before he did.

It seemed everyone was doing their best to turn her into the same red shade as her top. Maybe she didn't choose the right colour. At least with Gareth, she was able to speak. "Thanks," she whispered.

Buddy walked to Gareth, where he plopped down in front of him. The dog had snapped at the man earlier. Would he do it again? It was not in his nature. Under normal circumstances, he was affectionate with everyone. It could have been the trauma from the storm and the tides and having to swim to keep from drowning until Melissa grabbed him. "Looks like someone wants you to play with him."

Gareth lowered his gaze to the animal. "After our initial meeting, I'm not so sure."

"Lean down with the back of your hand facing him so he can smell you. I still think his reaction earlier was because he was scared."

He bent over and let his hand dangle near the little dog's face. Would the dachshund accept Gareth's olive branch? Melissa sucked in a breath and held it. Buddy leaned forward, sniffed, then licked the man. She exhaled, relieved, and more convinced Buddy's earlier behaviour was borne out of fear.

"I just hope he's not cleaning a spot so he can take a chunk out of me," Gareth joked.

Danielle entered the room carrying a charcuterie board laden with various meats, pâté, cheeses, pickles, and crackers. She placed it on the coffee table in the seating area then disappeared back into the kitchen. Moments later, she returned with plates, napkins and spreaders.

"I could have helped you with that," said Melissa.

"You're all right. Besides, you're supposed to be staying here in the warmth of the fire."

"I'm not an invalid."

"But you're on holiday. A healing holiday, not a working one."

Gareth cocked his head, and Mel knew the inevitable was

going to spew from his mouth. It was just a matter of when, and she dreaded that moment.

Danny disappeared once more and came back with a tray of cups, saucers and matching tea service. This was way too much. She'd gone too far.

"You didn't have to do all this," Melissa objected. "We're not Royalty."

Gareth chuckled.

"My bestie is alive and sitting in my house, thanks to this gentleman. Besides, the lasagna will take at least an hour. I thought you might want a snack and a hot drink. The guys will be joining us shortly. They've gone out to the workshop to check if the electricity is back."

"Still no juice in the shed," Gilles said when he came through the back door.

"You sure the main breaker didn't blow during the storm?" Danielle asked.

"I'm not stupid, sis. That was the first thing I checked." He bent down and removed his steel-toed workboots.

"He's right. I watched him," said Paul.

"Wash up and come on in the front room. We've got munchies to keep us going until supper is ready."

"Food? You don't have to tell me twice." Gilles turned to the sink and washed his hands, and dashed to the location of the snacks.

He sat on the couch near Gareth's chair, grabbed a couple of slices of Genoa salami and stuffed them in his mouth. "So what do you do for a living?" he asked as he chewed.

"Former soldier."

"Really? See any action?"

Paul entered the room and took a seat on the other end of the sofa.

Gareth stared at the floor.

"He might not be comfortable talking about it. Ever think of that?" Paul said.

"No. Didn't. Sorry about that, man. What brought you to

Percé?" That seemed an innocent enough question.

"Nothing special. Needed a break, so I'm working my way around the Gaspé."

There was more to Gareth's history than he was letting on. Still, for now, Gilles was willing to drop the matter, but before they went back to their prospective homes and jobs, he would have it figured out.

The five sat and made small talk, no one giving up much information about themselves in the company of their guest.

Melissa brought her cup of tea to her lips. The sound of a car engine similar to Iain's vehicle grew louder. She immediately dropped the piece of china, and it shattered on the floor — a puddle of brown liquid spread across the bamboo flooring. Buddy yelped and ran out of the room.

"What's wrong? You look like someone walked over your grave," said Danielle, sopping up the spilled tea with the stack of napkins from the charcuterie board.

"Th-that car. It sounds like Iain's."

"He doesn't know you're here. Besides, there are plenty of cars with noisy mufflers like that."

Gilles strode to the window overlooking the driveway. "Older model red Honda Civic? Performance package?"

Melissa began to shake.

"Who's Iain?" asked Paul.

"Her ex," Danielle explained and dropped it there.

"Did he hurt you?" Gareth turned to her.

She nodded.

"Not physically. Emotionally," Danielle interjected.

"You want us to deal with him?" Gilles inquired from across the room.

"No, I'll handle it. I didn't plan on bringing this into your home any more than I already have. I'll get rid of him." Melissa stood, sucked in a deep breath and walked to the door.

She flung it open as Iain was climbing the steps. "What do you want?" she snapped.

"What do you think? I want to apologize. I want you to

come home with me. Be married like we planned." He paused for a moment, then continued. "You look nice. New?"

"None of your concern. I spent *my* money, not yours. And after what you did to me, I wouldn't marry you if you were the last man on planet Earth."

The door closed behind her. Through her peripheral vision, she saw Gareth on her left, Paul and Gilles on her right. Where was Danielle? With any luck, inside calling the police.

"Isn't this cozy?" Iain sneered. "Doing all three of them, Mel?"

Gareth stepped forward, but Melissa placed her hand on his forearm and stopped him.

"That's rich coming from the man I caught in bed with another woman. Clothing was strewn from one end of the house to the other. It didn't take a rocket scientist to figure out you were screwing her."

Hot tears scorched Melissa's cheeks. She dashed them away with the backs of her hands. Her dirty laundry was aired in front of her teenage crush, her best friend's brother and the man who saved her life today. What more could go wrong?

Danielle appeared, holding a rolling pin in one hand and hitting the palm of her other one with it. "You heard her. She doesn't want anything to do with you. So why don't you climb back in your car and make like the birds." She took a step forward.

"Danny, don't," Melissa begged. "He's not worth an assault charge. He'd do it, too, just to get back at me."

"She's right. I'll have you charged if you lay one hand on me. That wouldn't do your reputation and your cushy little business any good." He flexed his fingers.

"Go back in the house, guys. I'll be fine."

"You sure?" Gareth put his hand on her shoulder and squeezed it gently.

Melissa nodded. The others went back inside.

"And shut the stinking door," Iain yelled. "This is between me and her."

The lock clicked when the door closed, leaving her on the verandah alone with her ex-fiancé, who needed to go.

"Nothing you can say will change my mind and take you back. What you did was so far out of line ... I can't even say the words. How would you have felt if you came in and found me in bed with another man?"

"Never happen. You won't even make love to me." He reached for her hand, but she snatched it back before he got a grip on it.

"You shattered my trust in you. Tore my heart out of my chest and ripped it into tiny pieces. I hate you for that."

"I want to make it up to you. Start over like it never happened." Iain put his hand in his jeans pocket and pulled out the engagement ring. "Please, give me another chance."

"Never. Now I suggest you leave. You're violating the restraining order I had taken out on you." Melissa had threatened it but never went through with it. He wouldn't know that, would he?

"You're wrong on that one. Restraining orders are only valid in the province they were sworn out in." A smirk formed on his face, and he stepped closer.

Melissa extended her arms and connected with Iain square in his collar bones and knocked him off-balance.

"You shouldn't have done that."

Her moment of bravado vanished. It was replaced with fear.

The door squeaked open and closed quietly. "The lady obviously wants nothing more to do with you, so why don't you climb back in your little car and return from whence you came. If you're not off the property in the next five minutes, the police will be involved."

Gareth leaned over and whispered in Melissa's ear, and she murmured back. "Hmm, from where I'm standing, it wouldn't do your reputation any good being arrested. Wouldn't do much for your job either. They frown on prison guards having criminal records. You'd be fired so fast you wouldn't know what hit you." He glanced at his smartwatch. "You're down to four minutes."

"It's not over, Mel," Iain stated as he scrambled for his car. He backed away from the house, spraying gravel as he spun the tires.

The tiny stones struck Gilles' truck with metallic tinks. At least it wasn't Paul's BMW getting damaged.

A warm arm encircled her shoulder. "Let's get you inside."

Twice in one day, this man came to her rescue. He really was her knight in shining armour.

Six

Fortin's Guesthouse, Percé, Québec

Gareth escorted Melissa back to the chair she occupied before their uninvited guest arrived. He sat on its arm and rubbed her back. Danielle brought her tea, this time in a mug instead of a fine china cup.

Paul leaned on the back of the armchair opposite. "What I don't understand is who told him where you were?"

"N-no clue." Melissa tightened her grip on the beaker. She already broke one dish today; she didn't want to destroy another. "I sure didn't tell him."

"Lasagna is in the oven," Danielle called from the kitchen.

"Fantastic. I'm starving," answered Gilles.

"When aren't you?"

"Enough. Melissa doesn't need to hear you two bickering." Gareth gave her shoulder a gentle squeeze before moving to the end of the sofa.

"It's all right. I don't mind. Really. Reminds me of home." Melissa held the mug in both hands, brought it to her lips, and sipped. Chamomile.

"You got that right. When you put all the Scott kids together, they could out-banter us Fortins hands down."

"You're exaggerating, Gilles," said Danielle.

"No, I'm not."

"Five of us and only two of you. We kind of had you beat, if only in numbers." Melissa smiled.

"Five?" Gareth said.

"Yup and the boys outnumbered the girls."

"Michael and Amy, the twins, were a couple of years older than us," Paul said, nodding at Gilles.

"Is he the oldest?"

"No, that would be Christopher. Then Roger, then Amy and Michael, then me."

"The baby of the family, eh?" A broad smile formed on Gareth's mouth, but his eyes didn't sparkle. A disconnect lay somewhere between.

"She played that every chance she got."

"I can believe it going up against four older sibs. Who is older, you or Danielle?"

Gilles rolled his eyes. "Danny. She's our baby. What about you, Gareth? Any brothers or sisters?"

By now, the savoury aroma filled the house.

"That smells delicious," said Gareth.

"Danielle is an excellent cook, even though she is my sister."

Gareth sighed. He dodged a bullet and hoped no one picked up on the fact he didn't speak about his family. The memories from Saint-Hyacinthe and later Valcartier remained too painful. Still. He was in the company of complete strangers. Even Melissa, for that matter. He was only in Percé for a few more days, then he would never see any of them again. All he had to do was avoid conversations of a personal nature. He had become quite skilled at that.

His right shoulder burned, likely related to his earlier heroics. Picking up Melissa and the dog and getting them into the boat. Rather than draw attention to himself by rubbing his injured extremity, he gritted his teeth and breathed through the discomfort. He had painkillers back at the hotel.

"The lasagna needs to sit for a bit before I can cut it, which will work out perfectly for the garlic bread I just tucked in the oven," said Danielle.

The sauce bubbled in the Pyrex baking pan beside a stack of plates on the island.

"Come and get started. The Caesar salad is on the dining room table. Wedges of lemon, too, if you want. There are still cold cuts and cheese. Speaking of which, will you bring the board out and put it with the greens, please, Paul?"

"Sure." He rounded the chair he stood behind and picked up the charcuterie plank from the coffee table.

"Why don't you sit at the end of the table, Gareth? We'll sit where we always did as kids," Danielle said.

Sweat dripped down the back of his neck. He would be on display with the spot chosen for him and unsure how long he could keep up the façade before his alter-ego escaped. Six chairs stood around the maple-topped table — one at each end and two on each side. Best deflect the discussion to the others. Melissa sat next to him on his left, with Paul beside her. Danielle and Gilles on his right. The chair Danielle occupied, was the logical choice for her; close to the kitchen island, so she could bring food over.

They passed the wooden salad bowl around, and everyone served their own helping. Soon afterwards, the lemon wedges made the rounds. Over the first course, the conversation picked up almost in the same place it had stopped earlier.

It was apparent the four had been friends for a long time. That could be Gareth's in to get them talking and leave him out of the exchange. "Mel is here on vacation, but what about the rest of you? Is this an AirBnB?"

"No, this is my sister's place. Used to be our parent's cottage. After Dad retired, he and mum moved down here permanently, and she opened it up as a guesthouse."

This was more than Gareth knew five minutes ago, but he still had unanswered questions.

"Our fathers worked together on the Québec side of the Ottawa River," Melissa said, nodding towards Danielle and her brother. Our house was on Elm Street, and theirs was around the corner on Rochester."

"My father worked downtown," said Paul. "We lived a block north of the Scotts on Primrose. I went to the same school as these guys."

"Summer holidays, we could each bring a friend when we came to the cottage. It was always us four," said Danielle.

"What happened to your parents?"

"Head-on crash on their way back here from Ottawa after New Years'. They'd come home for Christmas. Last time we saw them," said Gilles, his voice hitching.

"Sorry, guys, didn't mean to upset you." He put not just one of his size twelves in his mouth but both. Guilt washed over him. Gareth had only met the four people at the table with him earlier in the day. Not as strong as compared to his feelings about Afghanistan, but squeezing his chest, nonetheless.

"So, Gareth, how well do you know Ottawa?" asked Paul.

"Don't."

"So the neighbourhood we're talking about growing up in means nothing to you."

"No."

"Ever heard of LeBreton Flats?" Gilles asked.

What was this guy getting at? Trying to make Gareth share something about himself, he was not prepared to do? Still, the name sounded familiar.

"We used to go to the park there. Between it and the river is where the new Canadian War Museum is."

Beads of cold sweat formed on Gareth's forehead. "I need air." He leapt to his feet and dashed out the front door.

"I'll go after him," Melissa said, removing the napkin from her lap and placing it on the dining table.

Gareth stood on the verandah, holding the railing. She reached out to put her hand on his back and had barely touched him when he jumped.

"Yikes," he yelped and spun around. "You scared the living ..."

"Sorry, I came out to see if you were all right."

His eyes darted back and forth. He couldn't look straight at Melissa, and when he did, it was as if he stared through her.

"You helped me earlier today — twice, no less. Let me help you now." Melissa took his hand and guided him to the patio set. She turned one of the chairs so it faced Gareth and sat. "What happened in there?"

"What do you mean?" Now, in addition to his eyes darting back and forth, he twisted his whole upper body left and right and his head further in each direction. Panic filled the man.

"Come on. You know exactly what I'm talking about. You went pale when the car accident that killed Mr. and Mrs. Fortin was mentioned." Melissa reached out and took Gareth's hands in hers. "Then, when Paul brought up the war museum, you left the room like someone shot you out of a cannon. Tell me, please? It might help."

Gareth shook his head.

She rubbed her thumbs over his palms as she spoke. "You told me you were a soldier and not impressed when Gilles asked if you saw any action. You did, didn't you? That's why the mention of the word 'war' set you off."

"What are you? Freud? How dare you try to analyze me." He yanked his hands out of hers and went back to the railing.

Melissa stood. She grabbed Gareth by the arm and spun him around. "I'm not some little foo-foo princess you can dismiss so easily. I am tough. Trust me — growing up with four older siblings, I had to be. So, suck it up, put on your big boy pants and tell me."

He sighed and rolled his eyes. "You got me on that."

"Come back and sit down."

They returned to their chairs, and once again, Melissa gently took his fingers in hers.

"I'm not normally social — no idea why I accepted the dinner invitation. I would've been just as happy in my hotel room with takeout from one of the local restaurants. I think the only reason I did was that I wanted to see you again. I'm glad I was here to protect you from your ex."

"I don't need protecting, but I appreciate the gesture. Iain can be an idiot at times."

"Seen his type — controlling, manipulative."

"When did you serve?"

Gareth nodded. "Swear this goes nowhere, and I'll tell you."

"Cross my heart," she replied, gesturing as she spoke.

"My best friend, Normand Lévesque, and I enlisted in the army, never expecting to be called up for active duty. I was a bit older than him, but we grew up in the same street in Saint-Hyacinthe — kind of like you and your gang. Anyway, the last thing I did before we headed off to Valcartier was promise, swear to his parents, I'd take care of him. Keep him safe."

"And that didn't happen."

"No. Normand was driving our vehicle, which should've been able to withstand a roadside bomb. But it exploded at just the right, or maybe the wrong, time. Not a mark on him, but the blast killed him. We were in the Panjwayi District of Afghanistan. I failed. I broke my promise to them, and to this day, I've not gone home. I can't face Normand's parents."

"Gareth, I'm so sorry you're going through this." Melissa leaned forward and placed her palm on his cheek.

He bowed his head and pressed the heels of his hands into his eyes.

The door opened, and Danielle stuck her head out. "Lasagna is ready when you are."

"Give us a few, eh?"

"No probs. I'll cover yours and put it back in the warming oven until you want it."

Gareth lifted his head. "Don't ruin your meal because of me."

"I won't. Besides, you heard Danny. She's keeping ours warm for us."

His eyes were red, but it could have been caused by how he pushed his fists into them. There were no signs that tears ran down his face, nor had his body shuddered like he broke down. A psychiatrist she was not, nor a psychologist, but she was a friend, and friends stuck by one another.

"Maybe I should just go back to my hotel. I caused enough

trouble." Gareth stood and turned towards the railing.

"You'll do no such thing. And you've not done anything wrong. Why don't I bring our supper out here? We can have our meal away from them."

"What'd you make of that?" Gilles asked as he ripped off a piece of the garlic loaf. With his forearms resting on the dining table's edge, he watched his sister and Paul to gauge their reaction.

"Except that he was quiet, nothing seemed strange until you mentioned the War Museum, Paul," said Danielle.

"Yeah. Gareth did say he was an ex-soldier. Could be something to do with that. A touch of PTSD," said Paul.

"I knew there was something." The idea filled Gilles with a hint of glee. He shoved the bread in his mouth and chewed.

"I recognize that expression, bro'. You're up to something."

He raised his hands. "Who me?" he professed with an air of innocence, sending crumbs flying.

"Yes, you. Melissa is my friend, and Gareth seems like a decent guy. The two of them have hit it off, so back off. Hurry up and finish eating. The three of us will go for a walk and leave them to have their meal in peace."

Melissa returned to the dining room to have three sets of eyes staring at her. Inwardly, she squirmed. "Going to take our supper out to the porch so Gareth and I can eat out there."

"What was the dramatic exit all about?" asked Gilles.

"N-nothing," she stammered. Everything Gareth told her outside, he'd said in confidence. She wouldn't break his trust.

"The guys and I will go out when we're done eating. That way, you and Gareth can be alone to talk."

"Thanks, Danny."

Melissa donned oven mitts and took the two plates of lasagna towards the table on the verandah. Gareth was gone. "Gareth. Where did you go? Your lasagna's here. Come and eat before it gets cold."

No response.

She slumped into one of the chairs.

"Everything all right?"

"Don't know. Gareth has disappeared."

Danielle stuck her head back through the door. "Guys, go without me. I'm going to stay with Mel."

Melissa's vision was blurred by tears. On a disaster scale of one to ten, today had surpassed it. Today was at least an eleven.

"I sense you two have hit it off, but are you reading too much into the situation? I want you to be happy, but ..."

"You think because Gareth rescued me, I've fallen for him?"

"I wouldn't quite put it that way."

"Look. I appreciate his help. Out at the rock and when Iain showed up. I admit that. Gareth needs a friend, and I'm willing to be that friend." That name. Iain. It popped into her head again. Despite what he'd done to her, Melissa still loved him. Hated him, too.

"It's not so long ago that you kicked Iain to the curb."

"And with good reason."

"I'm not saying it wasn't. But I don't want you getting hurt again. Rebound relationships don't work. Never have."

"How did you get to be so smart?"

"Dunno. Now eat your lasagna before it gets cold. I'll wrap Gareth's up, and it can go in the freezer once it cools."

The screen door slammed shut behind Danielle. Why did Gareth take off like that? His behaviour worried her. Don't get too involved, she told herself, but she already was. He spilled his guts to her, which had to be hard for the man.

When the door closed behind Melissa, Gareth sprinted off the verandah and down the long driveway to the road. The sooner he escaped from Fortin's Guesthouse and the people in it, especially Gilles, the happier he would be. He didn't stop running until he reached the highway. By then, he was exhausted. Bent over, with his hands resting on his knees, Gareth tried to catch his breath. Slowly, his breathing returned to normal, and the pain in his chest from the exertion subsided.

He was far away enough now; the remainder of his return to his hotel could be done at a walk, albeit a brisk one. But what if they piled into one of the vehicles and came looking for him? No, he had to keep running. A glance over his shoulder revealed no followers. Every fifty feet or so, he paused and looked back again. Gareth found himself adopting the hunched war-time stance they had to maintain when they had no cover. Crouched over, he continued to run.

Periodically, he took advantage of signs and ducked behind them. With the number of hotels, motels and restaurants along the strip, there was no shortage of hiding places.

Gareth sighed when he reached the parking lot for the Motel Impérial. He darted towards the back of the hotel then rushed the rest of the way to his room. Once inside, he pulled the curtain shut and hung the "do not disturb" sign on the outside door handle.

In the small bathroom, he opened the bottle of prescription painkillers and dry swallowed two.

Seven

Fortin's Guesthouse, Percé, Québec

Melissa woke to the delicious aroma of frying bacon and brewing coffee. Her trip to Percé hadn't been the relaxing, healing time she hoped for thus far. Starting today, her vacation was returning to its original path — no more thoughts of men, past or present. She had no control over two of them because they were under the same roof; besides, they were childhood friends.

She crawled out of the comfortable bed and padded to the shower. Through the top half of the bathroom window, the overcast skies peered in on her. A closer inspection revealed the sun-kissed shades of a beautiful late spring day. What time was it? Melissa returned to the bedroom. The red numerals on the digital alarm clock read eight-fifteen. The sun had been up for hours. Did the cloud cover make the sky appear like a sunrise?

Once again, she put on her black skinny jeans. Instead of the cami she wore the previous day, she pulled on a t-shirt emblazoned with the name of the pub across the street from *jonathans* and draped a white hoodie over her shoulders.

Forty-five minutes passed before she walked into the open

plan living, dining, kitchen space. Had it not been for the aromas of breakfast cooking, Melissa quite likely would have stayed in bed even longer. Last night, she slept soundly — or at least thought she did.

"You okay, hun?" Danielle asked.

"Sure, why?"

"I thought I heard you crying."

"Don't remember that. A dream? I thought I slept great. I didn't wake up tired."

"Come and eat. The guys are out in the workshop, so we've got the house to ourselves."

Melissa sat, and within seconds, Danielle set a plate of bacon, eggs, mushrooms and hash browns in front of her, followed by a steaming cup of coffee. "You know, I'll be huge if you keep feeding me like this."

"No, you won't. You're out getting exercise every day, so you'll wear it off. Oh, I'm doing laundry today. Anything you want me to wash?"

"You don't need to do my washing. I'm a big girl. I can do it myself." Melissa's tone was sharper than she intended. "Sorry, I didn't mean to bite your head off. I guess you could throw in my clothes from yesterday. They got pretty messy."

"Leave them on the bathroom floor, and I'll grab them with the towels and sheets."

"Danielle," Melissa protested.

"Hey, I do anyway when paying guests are here, so don't worry. All part of running the business. What are your plans for the day?"

"Think Buddy and I will take a walk around the village. See how much has changed since the last time I was here."

"Sounds good. The weather is supposed to remain pleasant. You should be fine dressed like that."

"Yes, mother."

At that, both girls laughed.

"I need to buy dog food today. Any idea where I can get that?"

"The Co-op on the highway next to the gas station. The other side of the quay where the ambulance came for you and

Gareth."

"Thanks."

Melissa finished her breakfast in silence. Did she hope she might bump into Gareth in her travels? Perhaps if for no other reason than to ensure his well-being. After his runner last night, she wondered about his state of mind.

Wasn't it through her worry about someone that she first met Iain? He was on his motorcycle, and a car ran the red light and took him out. It happened outside *jonathans*, and she was first on the scene. Even went to visit him in the hospital a few days later. If only she had known how that act of kindness would be repaid.

She shook her head to flush those thoughts from her mind, drained the last of her coffee and took her dishes to the sink. Danielle was occupied with loading the dishwasher, so Melissa rinsed the egg off her plate before handing it, her mug and cutlery to her friend.

After ensuring she had plenty of stoop and scoop bags in the holder on Buddy's leash, the pair set out. Her first stop would be the store for dog food. She couldn't take him inside, so she hoped there was a shady place where she could tie him up to wait for her and that he would be safe.

Fluffy, white cumulus clouds floated in the azure sky. It was clouds like those that caused the trouble the day before, but those ones had patches of grey in them that weren't shadows. She'd pay more attention from now on.

More people wandered through the village today than since her arrival. As kids, they didn't spend much time in this part of the town. They ran and played on the bluff overlooking Percé Rock, on the beach or over the causeway to the rock at low tide.

Melissa found the grocery store Danielle mentioned with no problem. There was not much to choose from as far as places to leave her pet outside while she dashed in. Pillars protected the entrance, so she looped his leash around one and tied it.

It took some time to track down dog food and even longer to find a brand the fussy dachshund liked.

When she stepped out of the store, Melissa gasped in horror.

Buddy was missing. Did he slip his collar and run off? No. Had he, it and his leash would be on the ground. Why didn't she leave Buddy with Danielle until she finished shopping? If anything happened to him, she would never forgive herself.

Iain appeared from around the corner of the store's vestibule, holding Buddy in his arms.

Melissa was both relieved and angry at the sight. "Give me my dog, Iain," she demanded.

"Why, so you can leave him tied up outside?"

The smug expression needed to be knocked off the man's face, but she didn't dare be the one to do it. The restraining order was only a threat on her part, but if she slapped him, he'd prefer charges against her, sure as they both stood staring down one another.

"He's mine. I want him back" Melissa lunged towards him, but Iain stepped backwards, and she drove her knee into the pillar. Her leg buckled, and she clutched it. Despite the pain, she was determined to free her dog from her ex-fiancé, who continued to smirk and slowly step back from her.

"I'm calling the police," she said, pulling her smartphone from the back pocket of her skinny jeans.

"Is there a problem here?" a man in his late-forties early-fifties asked. Melissa spun around in the direction of the voice.

"Don't get involved, Harold," a woman, presumably his wife, said as she placed her hand on his forearm.

"Yes. I had to slip into the store, and while I was in there, my ex-fiancé", Melissa turned to Iain again, "took hold of my dog and won't give him back to me. We're here on holiday, Buddy and I, not the creep and I."

"Calm down, dear girl."

"I was going to run out of food for him later today. Yes, I should have left Buddy with Danielle while I came shopping, but returning to Fortin's Guesthouse so soon was not in my plans. I carry water and a collapsible dish for Buddy, so when we're out for long walks, he can have a drink." By now, Melissa was hysterical.

"Young man, I think you should give the lady back her dog." The man's voice was calm yet firm and full of authority.

Melissa looked from the stranger to her ex and back again. Finally, Iain passed Buddy over to her, snorted and turned on his heel. She wanted to thank the couple, the man most of all, for intervening but they were gone, too.

An emotional wreck, she collapsed on a planter built in between two of the pillars. Clutching Buddy to her chest, she bent over and wept.

Paul climbed out of the passenger side of Gilles' pickup truck at the gas station next to the small grocery. Between the cars pulled up into the bays facing the K-rails, the store's entire front was visible. "Hey, isn't that Mel over there?"

Gilles stopped taking the filler cap off and stared in the direction his friend mentioned. "Looks like her."

"I'll go see while you fill up and get the other bits you need. If I'm not back when you're done, pull around the other side."

What if he was mistaken? All he went by was the long mane of brunette hair.

He strode towards the front of the store. "Mel, what's wrong?" he asked gently.

She leaned against his shoulder. "I-Iain took B-B-Buddy and wouldn't give him b-back to m-me."

"But you have him, now," Paul said, stroking the dog's velvety coat.

Her breath hitched. "Only because a couple coming out after me intervened. Iain would have kept him. I know he would. Just to spite me."

A strong arm encircled her shoulder.

Eight

Motel Impérial, Percé, Québec

With no trace of Gareth since he disappeared the night of their Percé Rock experience, Melissa worried. What motel did he say he stayed at? The Impérial. The grocery store and gas station were too far away to make out the sign, but it wasn't much farther from them.

After breakfast the following day, she arranged to leave Buddy with Danielle, then she set out towards the village.

A cold wind blew in off the water this morning. Weather on the east coast could change without warning. Despite her hoodie and a long-sleeved t-shirt, and her ripped skinny jeans, Melissa shivered. The walk to the hotel took longer than she expected. She still had quite a distance to cover.

Paranoid Iain lingered in the town; she glanced over her shoulder every time she heard a car with a noisy exhaust. Relief washed over her when the vehicle was not his red Honda.

Inside the motel's reception, Melissa pulled off her sunglasses and perched them on top of her head. The lighting was dim, especially after coming in from outside. Letting her eyes grow accustomed to the lower light level, she stood by the door before walking to the unmanned desk. A sign taped to the counter indicated she should ring the bell if no one was available. Melissa slapped it with her right palm. A loud ding resonated.

A woman about her mother's age entered through a door at the back of the room. Most of these places, well, when she was a kid coming to Percé anyway, were mom and pop operations. Some likely still remained in the family's hands. "Puis-je vous aider?" the woman asked.

French. So far on this trip, she didn't encounter many people who spoke anything but English. This could be another throwback to those days. Melissa swallowed hard and began. "Can you tell me what room Gareth Young is in?"

The woman immediately switched language. "No. Privacy and all that."

Thankful she didn't have to press her rusty French into service, Melissa sighed with relief. "He's my friend. I've not seen him in a couple of days, and I'm worried about him. He told me he's staying here. Please. I think he might be in trouble."

"Gareth Young, you say. Trouble. In that case, let me look."

A few taps on the computer keyboard. "Young, Young. Ah, there. Last room. Take the boardwalk to the back of the hotel."

"Thank you."

Melissa followed the woman's instructions and soon found herself standing outside his room. Unlike the ones before, the room was almost at ground level because of how the terrain sloped. She stepped on the verandah, running the length of the building.

In front stood a classic motorcycle that resembled a Harley. She didn't recognize the name on the side of the fuel tank. The bike parked in this location didn't mean much. It could have been the only spot available when the rider returned, or the owner left it back here away from prying eyes.

The room behind the drawn curtains was in darkness. The 'do not disturb' sign hung at an angle from the doorknob, but even more worrying, the door was ajar — only a couple of inches, but still not latched and locked. Something was wrong. "Gareth," she called as she tentatively pushed the door open.

A wave of stifling heat and the sour smell of sweat hit her. Those were bad enough, but the room had been trashed. The table lamp on the nightstand visible from the door was tipped over, the shade askew. The mattress was standing on its side wedged against the box spring.

Gareth's wallet lay on the desk under the window, credit cards and cash spread over the surface. So far, only that made sense. If he had the billfold with him when he rescued her, it and its contents would have been soaked.

Melissa turned the heat off and changed the device to air conditioning mode before she went any further. Anything to try and bring down the temperature. Then she switched on a light and closed the door. The motel staff didn't need to see the room in this state. It would be back to normal soon enough, most likely without any permanent damage.

Melissa tiptoed around the foot of the bed. Gareth sat on the floor behind the upturned mattress's protection, his knees drawn to his chest and his head resting on them. His shoulders shook as he wept. She slid down beside him. That's when she noticed he held a photo of a soldier in uniform in his outstretched hand.

"Is that your friend?"

A pair of bloodshot, tear-filled eyes stared at her. No. Stared through her like she was not there. Melissa knew nothing about PTSD, but this room and Gareth's behaviour screamed just that. She pulled him into a hug. For the longest time, he rested in her embrace motionless but eventually wrapped his arms around her.

Melissa didn't know how long they stayed this way, but she had to break off the hold because he squeezed her so hard she couldn't breathe. They remained next to each other, neither one speaking. She took his left hand in her right, and they laced their fingers together. Knowing he wasn't dead or injured eliminated some of her worries, but his emotional state was tenuous at best.

He needed help, but this was not the time to broach the subject. Who knew if he had a stash of weapons and if he would use them on himself or her if he felt threatened? Better just to sit still and be there when this episode, if it could be considered that, passed, if it passed.

His pulse drummed through his fingers against hers. Over time the drumming slowed. That was a promising sign. "You're going to be all right," Melissa whispered. "I'm here with you and will stay as long as you want me to."

Again his stare bored through her, making her uncomfortable. Did he need medication? Was he on meds and had not taken them, and that's what caused this? She had so many questions and no answers. That frightened her, too.

Gareth shifted and stood. "What happened in here?"

"You don't know?"

"No."

Now what? Could Melissa tell Gareth her perspective? Should she even try? She sucked in a deep breath, exhaled and said, "I think you thought you were back in the war. You made this room into your bunker — your safe place."

At least this time, when he stared, he stared at her.

"Why don't we clean up and go do something. A walk on the boardwalk. Anything. Let's just get out in the sun and fresh air," she said. "I'll help."

It took both of them to heave the mattress back into position. With the lamp uprighted and its shade adjusted, the room appeared normal again.

"Why don't you take a shower, and I'll finish up here. Won't take me any time to make the bed ... once I find the bedding."

Melissa stripped off her hoodie, pushed up her sleeves, and tied her long hair up into a messy bun on the top of her head. She then opened the window over the table to help the heat escape but left the curtains drawn. The room had started to cool with the air conditioning on full blast, but the temperature was still uncomfortably hot. She found the sheets and bedspread wadded up in the corner.

A prescription bottle fell out of the bundle when she picked up the bedclothes. According to the label, the drug was Sertraline. She pulled her phone out of her back pocket and took a picture of the sticker. Once back at Fortin's Guesthouse, she would research the drug's name and its uses.

The shower was running, so Melissa took advantage of Gareth being occupied and popped open the container. No more than a dozen pills lay in the bottom. Cap returned to its proper spot; she placed the pill bottle on the desk.

Something round and dark was wedged in that same corner. She bent down. It was a helmet and under it was a leather jacket. Did she hang the coat over the back of the chair? No, best leave things alone. She didn't need him thinking she was snooping. The motorcycle outside had to be Gareth's. Once she gauged his mindset, she would ask.

As Melissa put the finishing touches on the bed, Gareth entered wearing nothing but a towel tied around his waist. He was slim and fit. A soldier, so of course, he would be physically fit. The lack of tattoos surprised her. Didn't all soldiers have at least one? None to be seen on any of the exposed skin.

Between his shoulder and his elbow, the marks were worse. It appeared that a chunk of muscle had been removed. From there to his wrist, they weren't as frequent or as red. Gareth mentioned he had taken shrapnel, and his arm was severely injured when he told her about the roadside bomb that killed his friend.

From her perspective, he didn't seem at all fussed that he paraded around almost completely naked in front of a girl he met a couple of days prior. Did he forget she was there?

Melissa stepped away but couldn't take her eyes off the man who yanked his duffel bag out of the closet and heaved the thing on the bed she just finished making. Jeans, boxers, socks, a white t-shirt, and a long-sleeved cotton shirt were placed beside the carryall. Was he going to drop the towel and get dressed in front of her? An audible sigh escaped her lips when he gathered everything up and went back into the bathroom, kicking the door closed behind him.

When Gareth returned, he appeared nothing like the man she found cowering behind the upturned mattress earlier. Research into PTSD and the prescribed drug would be in her future. Maybe even as soon as later that evening.

Air conditioning set to a reasonable temperature, they started for the door. "Don't leave your wallet and stuff there. It might get stolen if it's seen," she said.

Gareth returned his cards and paper notes to his wallet and jammed the billfold into his back pocket. The change that remained, he scooped into his hand and into a front one. He held the door for Melissa, then shut it tightly behind them.

"Nice motorcycle," she said.

"Yeah, not bad."

Despite being ninety-nine percent sure she knew the answer, she asked, "Any idea whose it is?"

"Mine."

"I didn't have you down as a biker."

"Doctor said the vibrations from riding would help my shoulder, so after a lot of research, I decided on this classic Norton."

"Never heard of them before."

"British bike originally, but they also had plants in North America."

"Your boots dried out, I see."

"Not totally, but much better than after I went in the water to rescue you. Stuffed the hairdryer down them and turned it on."

Melissa looked up at him and smiled.

His eyes lit up and laughter lines formed at their corners when he returned the expression.

Across the road from the motel stood a children's play park. Beyond that, the walkway leading to the boardwalk. However, crossing the highway that bisected the village proved a bit of a challenge. Finally, a car stopped to let them cross. Gareth took Melissa's hand, and they jogged to the other side.

They walked towards the plank-covered path, and he wondered what Melissa must think of him now. After her finding him a quivering wreck and trashing his room. He liked her. She was fun to be with. If only he could keep his emotions and memories in check. His hand pained, and he moved her to his left side and clasped her hand in his uninjured one. The surgeons did an excellent job repairing his arm, but there were some things he couldn't do as well or as long before the pain became too much to bear.

"Danielle told me there's a full moon tomorrow night. Why don't we go to the top of the bluff to watch it rise? She says they're spectacular. From what I remember as a kid, she's right."

Melissa wanted to spend more time with him. After everything, she still wanted to be with him. What she witnessed today was just a toe dipped into the bathwater. Gareth had far worse episodes. He came close to suicide more than once and attacked a fellow soldier, convinced the man was an enemy insurgent. That occasion could have seen him court-martialled. However, with the events in Afghanistan, his doctors and psychologists deemed that it wouldn't have served any useful purpose and might have made matters worse.

"Why not?" Something positive to look forward to. He needed more of that.

"What do you think of our village?" She looked up at him and smiled.

"Is it always this busy?"

"You think this is bad; wait until July and August. You can't move for tourists and walking out to the rock? Forget it. At least during the day. Middle of the night, you stand a better chance of being able to breathe and see something other than a wall of people."

Gareth led them to a bench. He stretched out his legs and tipped his head back. The early summer sun warmed his skin. Melissa still held his hand. Did he dare try to put his arm around her, or would that be too forward and scare her off. He didn't want to do that.

"When do you have to go back to work?" He asked the

question, afraid that the answer wouldn't be what he wanted to hear.

"I'm off indefinitely. My boss, he's such a sweet man, told me to take as much time as I needed and that my job would be waiting for me when I'm ready to go back."

"Decent of him. Where do you work? What doing?"

"Accounts receivable for a department store in Saint John, New Brunswick. It's one of a Canada-wide chain."

"And your ex-fiancé lives in the same city."

"Yes."

From the conversation at her friend's cottage the other night when the man showed up, the creep didn't deserve her. "Is he still causing trouble?"

"Uh, huh. Iain tried to take Buddy away from me yesterday. Thankfully, an older couple came out of the grocery store and intervened. Gilles and Paul were in the village to pick up some bits, so they took us home."

Gareth tensed at the torment this ex was giving her. "You don't deserve that. Promise me when you finally decide to go back; you'll take out a restraining order."

Melissa nodded.

"I found a prescription bottle in your room," she said.

Leaping from the bench and throwing his hands up, Gareth shouted, "What were you doing going through my things?"

She placed her hand on his left forearm, but he jerked it away as if she scalded him.

"I was not snooping, if you must know," she snapped. "It fell out of the wad of blankets when I picked them up to make the bed." Melissa stood and glared at him.

Would she drop it or ask questions? Questions he was not prepared to answer. If it was the bottle, he thought it was, the location where she found it seemed logical. At least she didn't go into the bathroom and see the array of bottles in there — only one prescribed by a doctor. The others were over-the-counter medications that supposedly helped with pain and joint inflammation — all of which likely had adverse interactions with one another.

"I'm sorry," he said.

Melissa laid her cheek against his chest, and Gareth wrapped his arms around her. She was good for him — possibly better than the drugs. He shouldn't have accused her of snooping.

Melissa sighed. With Gareth's reaction, he would have gone ballistic had she mentioned photographing it.

He was broken. Like the birds, she and her siblings tried to nurse back to health when they were younger, but his break was in his mind — not so easy to repair. Maybe even impossible. Still, there was something about him. Something that Iain didn't have, besides his time overseas and the trauma that came home with him.

Gareth took her hand, and they strolled along the boardwalk towards the pier. Neither spoke, but it was not an uneasy silence. They'd not walked far when Melissa stopped. "Let's get a selfie with Percé Rock behind us."

"You want a picture of me?"

"Yes. Why wouldn't I?"

Melissa set the camera to front-facing and snapped a photo. Satisfied it was positioned the way she wanted, she brought Gareth closer, held the iPhone up, so they were both in it and pressed the button again. She took a few more so she could choose the best one later and send a copy of it to Gareth.

Turning her back to him, Mel scanned through the photos. She scrolled back one too far, and the prescription bottle she photographed in the hotel room filled the screen. Quickly, Melissa moved back to the first picture taken outdoors. When she found the one she liked best, she made it the wallpaper on her phone.

She showed Gareth the pictures ensuring that she retained control of the smartphone. Once she searched online and found out what the medication was used for, she'd delete the image.

They walked, holding hands, along the shore towards the monolith, and Melissa rested her head against Gareth's upper arm. She stepped in front of him and turned, enveloping his waist in her arms before they reached the quay. If only something this simple would take away all his pain forever. In return, he wrapped his arms around her shoulders. The top of her head rested in the hollow between his shoulder and jawline. Did he? Was that a kiss she felt high on her forehead? Butterflies formed in her stomach.

When they arrived at the dock, a busker stood with his back to them, singing and playing his guitar. The man's case was open on the ground, and coins and paper notes littered the bottom. The two stopped and listened to the performance for a few minutes before continuing towards Percé Rock. They hadn't completely crossed over the cement roadway when Gareth released Melissa's hand, begging her to turn to see the cause. He jogged back and dumped the change from his pocket into the instrument case.

The gesture warmed her heart. As badly traumatized as Gareth was thanks to the war, he was altruistic. She hoped that over the coming days, she would see more of this side of him.

After dropping the coins, Gareth returned to Melissa's side, and they resumed their walk. The incoming tide forced them to retreat before the place on the cliff where Fortin's Guesthouse stood.

On their way back to the boardwalk, they encountered a pair of abandoned sandals— plenty of people milled around, on the beach or in the water. The shoes could have belonged to any one of them. Nonetheless, Melissa snapped a picture of the ownerless footwear.

Approximately halfway back to the jetty, Gareth boosted Melissa up onto the wall's flat surface that protected the wooden walkway from the waves. He stood on the gravel with his back to her.

Melissa's leg brushed against his right arm. A tingling sensation ran from his shoulder to his wrist — a far more pleasant feeling than the shooting and burning pains he experienced. Still, rather than taking a chance of that happening and setting him off into a psychotic flashback, he moved to her other side.

The incoming waves brought seaweed and other flotsam and jetsam to the shore and, when they receded, dragged the remnants away. The motion of the water soothed Gareth. Calmed him. Hypnotized him. Overhead, gannets and gulls circled. The warmth of Melissa next to him kept him centred. If he could go through life in a calm place with her by his side, he would die a happy man.

"I want to spend more time with you," he said, his voice husky.

"And me with you."

Melissa leaned down and wrapped her arms around Gareth's neck. Her face and those beautiful brown eyes were directly in front of his. Did he kiss her? Was this the right time? He didn't want to frighten her off, thinking he was too forward, but he longed to kiss her. Had since he first met her. Gareth reached behind her head and released the bun. She shook her head and let her hair tumble down over her shoulders.

He tipped his head and brushed his mouth lightly against hers. She didn't tense up or back away from him. That was an excellent sign. Once again, he touched his lips to Melissa's. As they kissed, he lifted her off the wall and held her in his arms.

In the back of his mind, he wished he'd met her sooner. Had spent more time with her. He had been in Percé since the first of the month and had to leave the day after tomorrow. He didn't find her until he prevented her from drowning on the sixth. It was not fair. She deserved better than that creep she was engaged to in a previous life. Could he be good enough for her with his mental problems?

Nine

Percé, Québec

Breathless from his kiss, something Iain's kisses never did to her, Melissa struggled to regain her composure. "Let's do something tonight." The idea made perfect sense since they both agreed they wanted to spend more time together.

"Sure. What? You're the resident expert."

Melissa thought for a moment. A meal out would be fantastic, but could Gareth handle being in a public place? Maybe a takeaway back at his motel? No, that might give him the wrong idea. She still had to look up the prescription she found earlier. Best to leave their next encounter until after supper.

"You said the full moon is tomorrow night, and we've made plans to watch it come up and the sun go down, or should that be the other way around?"

"Why don't we go out to the rock tonight since the tide will be out? If I remember right, it should be about eight o'clock. Still not quite a full moon, but close."

"You really want to go out there after what happened the last time?"

"You'll be with me. I'll be safe."

Gareth smiled. "But will I?"

Melissa swatted his arm playfully.

"Hey, it's early. Plenty of light left. Why don't I take you out on the bike?"

"Are you sure?"

"Come on, let's go." Gareth grabbed her hand, and they started back to his hotel.

The mere thought of getting on a motorcycle terrified Melissa. What if the same thing happened to them as did Iain? He suffered a broken leg, numerous cuts and bruises, and a significant case of road rash when the car hit him. After he got out of the hospital, he never rode again. Unsure if she wanted to go through a similar situation, she had to go back to Gareth's hotel because she left her hoodie behind. "What about a helmet?"

"Carry an extra."

"You really are prepared." Inwardly, she cursed him for his preparedness.

"Was a Boy Scout long before I became a soldier."

Gareth was unhappy with Melissa's footwear, but her running shoes were better than sandals or, worse yet, flip-flops. He picked up his matte black three-quarter helmet and leather jacket and then dug through his duffel bag for something for her. "Put this on over your hoodie. You might not think so walking, but you'll be cold when you're out there at speed. Oh, and stick your phone in there," he said and pointed to the buttoned pocket of the coat.

She pulled up her hood and slipped on the denim garment. The sleeves were too long, but at least she had more protection than she did before.

He lifted a white full-face helmet down from the shelf of what served as the closet area and handed it to her. Gareth then hooked his pair of aviator sunglasses to the neck of his white t-shirt before putting on his coat. The last thing he did before they left the room was grab his head protection.

Outside, he straddled the bike and kickstarted the engine

before climbing off and knocking down the rear footpegs with his boot. "Make sure you keep your feet on these," he instructed. "The exhaust pipes get hot. I don't want you getting burned."

Melissa nodded

"Once your helmet's on, I'll adjust the strap so it fits properly." Once he had her fitted, he donned his sunglasses, zipped up his jacket and strapped his headgear in place. "To get on, put your hand on my shoulder, step up on the peg with your left foot and swing your right one over. When we're moving, wrap your arms around my waist and move with me."

Gareth climbed back astride the Norton and moved forward, giving Melissa more room to mount. She gripped his leather jacket, where he said and managed to situate herself on the seat behind him. He dropped the motorcycle off the stand and walked it back from the verandah before engaging the gears and heading towards the street.

She squeezed him tightly and rested her head against his back, both actions indicating she was terrified. Maybe suggesting a ride wasn't such a good idea. While they waited for the traffic to clear, he patted her hand, and she loosened her grip.

When he was alone, Gareth took chances. With Melissa with him, he would be careful. Gareth eased onto the highway with a sweeping right turn. They wouldn't go far unless she became more comfortable.

Melissa relaxed, knowing Gareth wouldn't take any risks. She opened her eyes. Sun glinted off the Gulf of St. Lawrence. In some cases, it was so bright it blinded her. Cottages and permanent homes dotted the land between the road and shore.

She let go with one hand and wiped her sweaty palm on her thigh, then repeated the process with the other — her confidence growing by the minute. Then they took a curve at full highway speed. She raised her feet and dug her knees into his waist, all the while hugging him tighter.

The wind buffeted her jean jacket and made the fabric flap

and pushed against her legs, too. But the vibrations! Her entire body buzzed from the soles of her feet, through her backside to the top of her head inside the helmet. She understood why the doctor recommended Gareth buy a motorcycle.

Burrowed in behind him, Melissa breathed in the scents of leather and spicy body wash. Those pleasant aromas were periodically overwhelmed by unpleasant odours. The exhaust fumes from one of the vehicles they met were so pungent, she gagged.

They had not been gone long when he slowed and turned left down a narrow side road. Melissa peered around and over his shoulder but didn't see anything of interest. Not until a lighthouse's red roof appeared did she discover the reason behind coming this way.

Gareth stopped the bike on a driveway to nowhere and, using sign language, instructed her to dismount. He shut off the engine and engaged the kickstand before climbing off himself.

Melissa removed her helmet and shook her head. Her hair was a tangled mess from the wind whipping it behind her. She tried running her fingers through her tresses, but the knots were too tight. From where she stood, Percé Rock couldn't be seen. Île Bonaventure scarcely showed over the landscape in front of her.

Helmet removed and sat on the motorcycle's seat; Gareth took hold of Melissa's hand. "What did you think of your first ride? Figured that was the case when you grabbed my waist in a death grip."

Gareth placed his other palm on her cheek. His touch was gentle and warm. He took the helmet from her and put it with his. With his palms on her face, he guided her mouth to his and kissed her. She melted into his body. His kisses were electrifying, and once again, butterflies formed in the pit of her stomach.

Sooner than she wanted, he broke the embrace and moved behind her. Gentle tugs pulled on her long hair. "That's going to hurt when you try to brush it out later. Sorry. You needed a leather braid holder. I would have wrapped your hair for you. Guess before we go out again after this, I'll have to invest in one." He kissed the top of her head then moved to her right side. They walked hand in hand to the end of the gravel lane.

In addition to the lighthouse, two houses stood off to their right. Would the owners come out and tell them to leave? Phone the police on them? Another property with a neatly manicured lawn was behind them on the opposite side.

They returned to the bike, but Gareth led her towards the red-roofed buildings instead of getting back on. They strolled down the road as far as they could. Vehicles parked around both houses and a humongous dog lay in the grass gnawing on something. The crackling of splintering bone soon told them what the animal chewed.

Discretion being what it was and not wanting to be a chew toy for the enormous canine, the two backed away before turning around and dashing back to the motorcycle. Melissa unfastened the denim jacket and her hoodie and adjusted them so her hair was inside under the inner layer next to her t-shirt. As they put their helmets on, they joked about the size of the beast in the yard. "He didn't come after us, which is a good thing. He was as big as Cujo, if not bigger," Melissa said.

"How do you know the dog's a male?"

"Just a guess."

This time, Gareth had the bike running and off the kickstand before she climbed up on the footpeg, placed her hands on his shoulders and swung her leg over. Once she was in position, he started back.

A rest area housing a playground and washrooms nestled in the space between the beach and the thoroughfare. A boardwalk ran on that same side until the water got too close.

On her left, a single rail line drew alongside them. The rusted rails indicated they had not been used in quite some time. Farther down the highway, Gareth turned, and they rode up to the train station. It, too, looked abandoned. When Melissa tried to book her way here, the trains no longer ran to Percé, and the terminal was well outside the town's border.

Back on the highway for only a few moments, Gareth pulled into a marina. The building along the shore appeared to be an old cannery. Out front stood picnic tables with patio umbrellas. The roadside sign read LA VIEILLE USINE. Identical wording but in a different font graced the upper wall. There was more lettering on the billboard, but it was smaller and too difficult to read. Her guess that the structure was a former canning operation could have been right.

He parked the bike, but they took their helmets with them when they went for their walk. The place was too busy to risk leaving them behind. A covered pedestrian walkway stood beside the bridge. They walked to about the middle and gazed out over the narrow river. Gareth eased behind her, wrapped his arms around her waist, and Melissa leaned into him.

Yes, it was too soon after her break up from Iain, but with the way this man made her feel, she knew she was falling for him. Huge. Were his feelings the same? He had kissed her. Hugged her. They stood here now, him holding her.

The sharp tang of fuel mingled with seaweed and dead fish. Boats of various sizes bobbed on the waves from their moorings on either side of the inlet. Seagulls hovered overhead, squawking. Purple martins and swallows dived to catch bugs.

When Gareth finally indicated they should leave, they followed a narrow road dotted with newer and centuries-old houses. In the gaps between the trees and buildings, Percé Rock remained hidden. Only water and the gray-green lump of Île Bonaventure showed themselves.

The road joined the highway in a backwards Y junction. Not much beyond that, Melissa spotted a small white dot on the top of the bluff near the water, which had to be Fortin's Guesthouse. She concentrated on the speck as they continued their ride, and it disappeared from view, obstructed by the oaks and maples.

Windrows of the first cut of hay filled a farmer's field. The fresh scent took her back to her childhood. On her mother's side, one of her uncles farmed about two hours southeast of Ottawa, and sometimes her entire family went and helped with the haying. Melissa only recalled going twice. The uncle died after that, and her aunt sold the farm. Whether bad memories or too much work, she didn't know, but that was her aunt's decision to make.

After they crested the hill and navigated some corners, the nondescript speck reappeared, but was larger now. It turned out to be a streetlight. There was no signage on Danielle's guesthouse. Whatever she saw before had to have been a light fixture, a transformer, or the sun catching a metal roof or even have been a road sign.

Just before another curve and between two hydro or telephone poles — she couldn't tell the difference — the white dot appeared again. Off to her left, looming over a white garage, was Mont Sainte-Anne. Still, Percé Rock remained hidden.

The iconic pierced rock showed itself when they reached a rest area at the top of a hill on a corner across the road from a campground. Gareth turned in and stopped near the railing. They sat briefly with the bike idling before he pulled back on the highway, and they travelled a bit farther. A hotel and restaurant parking lot had even better views, so he drove in there and, this time, shut off the motorcycle's engine.

Melissa took it as her cue to climb off. As she walked towards the cliff face, she removed her helmet. From here, despite knowing its massive size, the rock looked small. She took her phone out of her pocket, switched to the camera function and snapped pictures.

"Be careful. You're getting close to the edge." Gareth pulled her back a few steps to keep her from falling. To their left, there was a wooden rail fence, so he steered her in that direction. He couldn't bear it if something happened to her when she was in his care. That was not the correct term, although he felt like he was looking after her, protecting her.

Melissa was beautiful. She was the first person to bring out the nurturing side of him. His feelings went deeper than that, though. He was falling in love with her. No more falling. He had. But what about his flashbacks and meltdowns? He couldn't expect her to put up with them daily. It wouldn't be fair.

Gareth wished he could stay grounded and in the present when she was with him as he had since they first climbed on the bike. He blew up at her when she mentioned finding his prescription bottle.

Sometimes, he likened himself to Dr. Jekyll and Mr. Hyde with the way his mood swings propelled him from one persona to another. He was not an evil person. Never had been. Even now, he didn't consider himself that way. Just his mind was so screwed up since losing Normand in Afghanistan, he was evil at times.

Melissa witnessed one of his psychotic breaks, and it didn't frighten her, or if it did, she pretended otherwise. She sat with him through it. Didn't cast judgments — she was there as his friend. Was that all she saw him as? Nothing more? The few occasions he kissed her said differently. What would happen after they parted company? Would they stay in touch? He hoped so. It would be a shame to lose contact with her.

He eased behind her, wrapped his arms around her waist, and rested his chin on her shoulder. A few stray strands of her hair tickled his nose, but he didn't move. He nuzzled his way to her bare neck and placed soft kisses on her skin.

Content to stay like this for as long as she wanted, Gareth waited for Melissa to decide she was ready to leave. The sun beating down on his black leather jacket made him uncomfortably warm, but once they were moving again, he'd cool down. If it meant spending time cuddling with her, it was worth every millisecond of discomfort.

She played with her phone and brought it up to take a selfie. Gareth still didn't fathom why she wanted pictures with him. When she shifted to put the rock behind them for another shot, he moved in unison with her. Melissa pouted her lips, and he planted a kiss on them. At that same instant, she pressed the shutter button on the camera.

Farther down the road, a campground stretched along the space between the highway and the shore. Charcoal barbecues filled the air with a woody scent. The mouthwatering aroma of hotdogs grilling wafted as they rode past. Near the end of the camping area, one of the campers had their fire pit going.

Beyond that, the smells returned to the brackish tang of the Gulf of St. Lawrence. The closer they drew to the village of Percé, the more motels and cabins dotted the landscape on the left. The sandy shore on the right wasn't entirely white but a pale gray. The traffic was heavier now. Vehicles of all shapes and sizes, pedestrians and bicycles jockeyed for position. Melissa chewed on her bottom lip. The street was not nearly as busy when they took off earlier in the day.

The highway swung away from the water enough that now, accommodations and eateries dotted both sides. The aromas coming from the kitchens, while delicious smelling, didn't compete with the grilling hotdogs from back at the campground.

Fortin's Guesthouse was no longer a dot on the horizon. The white walls and red roof were clearly visible. Gareth drove on past the motel where he was staying, but when he turned on Rue Mont Joli, she realized he was taking her back to Danielle's.

Before he shut off the Norton, the bike engine's rumble brought Danielle, Paul and Gilles out to see who arrived on a motorcycle.

Melissa dismounted and took off her helmet. "Where do you want me to put it?"

"Hang on to it for now. Same with the jacket. I'll get them both from you later."

"We're still on for tonight?"

"Wouldn't miss it. See you about seven?" Gareth said, smiling. She was sure his smile reached his eyes this time, but behind his aviator sunglasses, it was impossible to tell.

He stretched and kissed her on the cheek, then kickstarted the bike and drove off.

"Gareth not staying? He's more than welcome," said Danielle.

"No, but he's coming back later. Low tide, so we're going out to the rock."

"After the last time, you still want to go out there?" Gilles asked. By now, he and Paul stood next to Melissa.

"I didn't have you down as a biker babe," said Paul.

"I didn't have me down as being one either." Melissa pulled her knotted mess of hair forward over her shoulder. It was in such a state she doubted a comb would ever get through it. "I'm going to shower before supper. Maybe if I start now, by this time next year, I'll have my hair in some form of normality."

Before getting on a motorcycle again, she would ensure her hair was at least in a ponytail or under her clothes. She still wanted to look up the prescription medication she found in Gareth's hotel room, but it would wait.

Inside, Buddy ran to meet her. He stood on his back legs and begged her to pick him up. Melissa obliged. It hadn't been much of a holiday for him. The long bus and train ride in a crate. The storm. Iain's attempted dognapping led her to leave the wee dachshund back at Danielle's today. She'd make amends tonight and take him with her and Gareth out to Percé Rock.

Cuddling the animal, she worked her way through the cottage to her room and the ensuite. She set him down on the bathmat by the soaker tub. Melissa undressed and climbed under the soothing spray. Her body still buzzed from having spent most of the afternoon on Gareth's Norton. Hair shampooed twice, conditioner applied and rinsed followed by a leave-in product, she finished in the bathroom.

She should wear something different tonight, but what? In addition to their walk to the rock, they would stay out and stargaze. Melissa opted for her black skinny jeans again, but this time with a beige, bulky knit turtleneck and his jean jacket over top of it. She still had the wool blanket from the paramedics, so she would take that with her as well.

Dressed, except for the sweater, Melissa flopped at the dressing table. She immediately jumped off. Her butt hurt. Until now, she had only sat on the motorcycle, and its vibrations masked any pain she might have had. She gingerly settled again and started on her hair. Towel drying would only make things worse, so once she unwrapped it, she bent over, letting the dark brown tresses fall forward and brushed from her hairline towards the tips. The process was more difficult than anticipated. She yelped when the brush got caught in a massive knot, and she tugged too hard.

Ten

Fortin's Guesthouse, Percé, Québec

Danielle knocked on the door and poked her head in. "You okay?"

"Just my hair. What a tangled mess."

"Let me give you a hand." She moved behind her friend and used her fingers to help separate the knotted strands. "You and Gareth, you're getting close."

"We-we're just friends," said Melissa.

"I think it goes deeper than that. Be careful, won't you? You don't know much about him other than what you told me. I don't want to see you hurt again."

"I'm going to sound like a teenager with this statement, but he's kissed me twice now."

"See what I mean? You're moving too fast. But the kisses? Good?" Danielle's smile reflected in the dressing table mirror.

"Electrifying. So unlike Iain's. I've never experienced anything like that before."

A twinge of envy coursed through Danielle. No one ever kissed her like that. "Wow." Unable to come up with something else to say, she picked up the hairbrush and ran it through Melissa's hair. The knots, except for a few particularly stubborn ones, gave way to the bristles, and soon her friend's hair was tangle-free.

Danielle hopped on the foot of the bed. Melissa turned around on the stool. "I have a confession to make. When you spilled your guts about catching Iain cheating on you, I invited Paul and Gilles to come."

"I thought so."

"Now, don't get mad. Hear me out. You had a massive crush on Paul back when we all lived in Ottawa. I did, too. He's still single, so I hoped perhaps you and he might …"

"Danny! He never showed any interest in me. He followed you like a lost puppy. It hurt, but I survived."

"Well, there's where I need to confess another thing. I went with Paul briefly."

"You what?" Melissa's eyes widened. "How come you never told me until now? How come I never found out on my own?"

"We made sure to be careful when we hung around with you or your family. Neither one of us wanted to hurt you. We didn't last long. In the end, we agreed to break up. Didn't want to ruin our friendship or those of our friends."

"I thought we were friends. How could you do that to me?"

"Mel, please. We didn't plan it. It just happened. I'd never intentionally do anything to hurt you."

"I think you better leave me alone for a while. I need time to take in all this."

When Danielle walked by Melissa, she bent down and kissed the top of her friend's head.

Melissa leaned against the closed door and sighed. Her life unravelled yet again. When did Danny and Paul start seeing one another? Was it one of the times the Scotts helped with the relative's haying? That made sense. Or right under her nose, and she was too stupid to realize? It was so sneaky. Danielle wasn't like that, or so she thought.

Did she have pushover tattooed on her forehead? Iain's cheating came as a complete surprise. He must have been adept at covering his tracks because she never suspected a thing.

Gareth came with his own set of problems. Dead friend, terrible war memories, and PTSD in all likelihood. The drugs. Melissa took her phone out of the jean jacket pocket where she kept it during the entire ride and scrolled through the pictures until she found the one she took of the prescription bottle.

Her tablet was on the nightstand. Once the device powered up, she opened the browser and typed in the drug's name — Sertraline. The medication was an anti-depressant and used to treat post-traumatic stress disorder. Some of the effects mirrored what she saw in Gareth's hotel room — agitation, sweating, hallucinations, and the list went on. The most frightening was that it could cause suicidal thoughts — quite the oxymoron. Take an anti-depressant so you could get further depressed and think of doing yourself in.

Danielle pushed the front door open. "Paul, I need to talk to you."

He and Gilles sat at the patio table at the end of the verandah. "What's up?" he asked as he stood and walked towards her.

She quickly bundled him inside the house away from her brother and led him to the kitchen. "Mel knows about us," she whispered.

"How?"

"I told her. At first, I was trying to set you and her up together on this trip. She needed someone steady after what that rat did to her."

"And what else did you tell her?"

She leaned on the island and sucked in a deep breath. "That you and I were a couple for a while." There, she said it. Confessed to both parties.

"Not quite how I remember those events, but Mel's vulnerable enough at the moment to believe almost anything. How did she take it?"

"Not well."

"Your timing sure stinks. I'll give you that." Paul walked away.

"Where are you going?"

"To talk to Mel. Damage control."

Danielle followed him with her eyes until he disappeared around the corner.

"Mel, it's me, Paul. Can I come in?"

"Go away," she yelled through the closed door.

"I'm not leaving, so you might as well let me in."

Footsteps crossed the room, and the lock clicked. Melissa opened the door. "What do you want?"

"To talk." He brushed his way by and sat on the bed. "Danny told me what she did. The matchmaking scheme for this week. Her and I dating at one time. I think she did that more to torment me than anything back then. I liked her and knew she had a crush on me. She knew you had a crush on me, too."

"So why did you do it?"

"Come here and sit down." Paul patted the mattress.

When Melissa joined him, he took her hands in his. At least if he had hold of her, he could prevent her from lashing out like a cat with her long fingernails.

"I believe she embellished a little — no, a lot. I never thought of us as a couple. Sure we hung out with no one else around. I never held her hand. Never kissed her. Didn't love her. You were the sister I never had. I never thought of you as anything else. Maybe because we grew up so close to each other. Our families. Sometimes, it was hard to tell where one ended, and the next one started."

Tears ran down Melissa's cheeks, and Paul brushed them away with his thumbs.

"Danny is sorry for telling you and making it look like we dated. I hate what Iain did to you in a brotherly kind of way." He hugged her, kissed the top of her head and closed the door behind him when he left.

The atmosphere during supper that evening was strained. Gilles picked up on the tension in the room as soon as he came in to eat. He cast his eyes around at everyone. His sister plated the leftover lasagna on the island and brought it over two plates at a time.

What went on since Mel got back from the ride with Gareth? Things appeared to be all right until Danielle called Paul indoors. Whatever happened occurred after that.

He was not going to let it spoil his meal. His plate no sooner hit the table than he wolfed down the food and snatched a piece of garlic bread from the basket. Between mouthfuls, he spoke in an attempt to cut through the atmosphere.

"Gareth's got quite the motorcycle. Did you know he had one, Mel?"

"Not until today," she replied, not lifting her head.

She ate a couple of bites of the pasta then pushed her plate back. "Sorry, not hungry."

"Can I have it?"

"I don't care. Do what you want." Melissa placed her napkin on the dinner table and left the room.

"What's going on?" Gilles asked once Mel was out of range.

"N-nothing," Danielle said.

"That's a load of bull. We were all getting along. Talking, laughing, and reminiscing about coming here as kids every summer. Now the three of you can't bear to look at each other."

"Everything is all right. It will pass," said Paul.

The rumble of the approaching motorcycle ended the conversation.

Eleven

Fortin's Guesthouse, Percé, Québec

Melissa emerged from the bedroom with Gareth's jean jacket over her shoulders, Buddy and a wool blanket tucked in one arm. "I'll be late. Don't wait up." She strode to the front door and out before anyone had the opportunity to speak.

"Let's go," she said to Gareth when she reached the bottom step.

He removed his helmet, buckled the strap and hung his headgear over the handlebar. "Are you all right?"

"I don't want to talk about it." She set Buddy on the grass, and they started down the driveway. The dachshund weaved back and forth in front of them, his nose to the ground. Periodically, he lifted his head and sniffed the air.

Gareth placed his palms on Melissa's shoulders and turned her, so she faced him when they were at the end of the lane. The heat radiating from them warmed her. Tears burned her eyes and blurred her vision. One salty tear escaped and ran down her cheek. Gareth wiped the droplet away with his thumb then kissed the spot on her face. He drew her into a hug and held her to him.

"Come on. If we're going to see the sunset and low tide

and the not-quite full moon, we best go," she said and tugged on Buddy's leash to get him moving.

The sky's colours progressively changed to red and orange, with streaks of purple clouds slashed across it as the sun dipped behind Mont Saint-Anne.

Melissa took the lead to the observation platform. They stood in silence as the skies darkened and the moon crested the horizon. Tomorrow night, the orb would be perfectly round, but now one side remained flat but still beautiful. Starting out a shade of pink as it peeked over the Gulf of St. Lawrence, the sphere turned more orange as it rose in the sky.

Paths crisscrossed the fields, but rather than stumble in the darkness on the uneven ground, she doubled back to the road she used to go to the rock. To make better time, Melissa scooped up Buddy. The tide was receding when they reached the staircase to the shore.

A few people walked along the beach in the immediate area, but they were alone when they turned to walk towards Percé Rock. Melissa let Buddy down but kept him on his leash. She wouldn't make that mistake again.

Water still covered the causeway. Not much, only about an inch, but enough to soak their feet. They could wait it out here.

A nearby boulder provided plenty of room for them both to sit on. Gareth took her by the hand and led her to it. She sat, but he remained standing in front of her. "Will you tell me now why you're so upset?"

Melissa sighed, drew her knees towards her chest and wrapped her arms around them. "Something Danielle did."

"Must be bad to put you in this kind of mood."

She couldn't tell Gareth everything. What happened was history. Each one told a different version. Which one was true, and why did their actions bother her so much? "The guys being at Fortin's Guesthouse these same two weeks is a setup."

"Hmm."

"Hmm, all you like, but Danny was trying to play matchmaker and fix Paul and I up together all because when we were kids, I had a massive crush on him."

Gareth chuckled.

"What's so funny?"

"You getting bent out of shape over your friend's attempt to set you up with a guy. Guess I threw the proverbial spanner into that."

Melissa smiled. She liked the idea that Gareth scuttled Danielle's plan. The combined veil of anger and sadness lifted.

By now, the tide receded, and they walked across towards the near-vertical cliff face. High above them, nesting gannets communicated with one another in short bursts of sound. Stars twinkled overhead. The night was magical. Perfect even.

"How long before we have to go back? I'm an inland boy and not up on tides and such."

"After midnight."

Gareth pulled Melissa into his arms and kissed her. If only the night could last forever. If only he could stay. If only he could spend the rest of his life with the woman in front of him. A lot of ifs, but he'd fallen for her and hard.

"Before it gets too dark and we can't find our way to the mainland, what say we start back."

"I know my way, and the moon is bright enough to guide us."

"You know your way. You who got stranded out here by the incoming tide and the storm."

"We'll go back."

This time Gareth took the lead, and he guided them back to the observation deck, which overlooked Percé Rock. He took the blanket from Melissa and spread it on the ground, sat down, and patted the spot next to him with his left hand. "See that bright star?" He pointed to the right of the moon and higher. "Jupiter and on the other side, not quite as high is Vega."

"How do you know all this?"

"The fighting didn't stop just because the sun went down. You had to learn the night sky and quickly if you wanted to stay alive. Here, lie back and look. It's amazing how many stars are actually visible when there's no light pollution."

Melissa laid down beside him, her shoulder lined up with his. Buddy crawled in between the two of them.

Gareth reached out and took Melissa's hand, then stared back at the heavens. He turned his head and smiled at her before returning his attention to the dark skies above him. "Recognize any constellations?"

She paused before answering. "The Little Dipper?"

"How about that one shaped like a W? You might need to turn around to be able to see."

"Nope, not familiar."

"Would you believe me if I said that's Cassiopeia?"

"It is?"

"Yup ,and that bright star down and to the left of the moon is Saturn. If we're lucky, the International Space Station will go over. I didn't check the schedule and duration of visibility. Mind you, with my luck, it will likely be over the Southern Hemisphere."

Gareth rolled up on his side and propped himself up on his elbow. He stroked Melissa's cheek with his other hand. What he had to tell her was not easy, so he needed to say it now and have the unpleasant task over. "Unfortunately, I must go back to Valcartier the day after tomorrow."

"Why?"

"I only had ten days leave. I left the base on the first and am due back on the tenth." He expected her to be bitter because he hadn't been upfront with his plans.

"I guess I don't know enough about the military and how it all works."

"I applied for a transfer to go back to Afghanistan the year after my first tour ended. They refused. My injuries were too recent and too severe to let me go back to active duty. Even now, I'm still under the care of the army medics as well as a couple of civilian ones before they set me loose on the world."

"Then we'll have to spend as much time together as possible."

Those words. Melissa was not mad. She wanted to be with him. He lifted her head and slipped his arm under it, and stroked her jawline. Melissa cuddled closer and put her head on his chest.

Buddy shifted and ended up on top of Gareth, close to Melissa's face. He petted the dog with his other hand — the velvety ears so soft and delicate beneath his fingers — the sleek coat.

Typically, this was the worst time of day for Gareth. Nighttime brought disturbing dreams, hallucinations and paranoid episodes. Here, tonight with Melissa in his arms, contentment filled him for the first time in many years. He couldn't let this girl slip away from him. He must have dozed off, comfortable with himself and his circumstances. It was going on four o'clock in the morning when he opened his eyes and checked his smartwatch. "Mel." He shook her shoulder. "We fell asleep."

"Mm, what time is it?" she asked, her voice sleepy.

"Late. I have to take you back." He scrambled into a sitting position.

Melissa yanked out her phone and stared at the lock screen. They spent almost the entire night under the stars. Waking up in Gareth's arms was heavenly. She couldn't describe her emotions any better way. Reluctantly, she sat up. By now, Gareth stood over her. He pulled her to her feet, then swept her into an embrace and planted another of those electrifying kisses on her lips.

"Good morning, beautiful," he said after the kiss ended.

"And to you, handsome." She wrapped her arms around his waist and leaned against him. Armed with the knowledge they only had today together, she was loath to let go of the man. With the tender yet tight hug he held her in, she knew her feelings were reciprocated.

Heads bowed, they began the walk back to Fortin's Guesthouse. Despite telling Danielle, Gilles and Paul not to wait up for her, at least one, if not all three, would have. The inquisition would start the moment she walked in the door.

"Do you want me to come in with you?" Gareth asked when they reached his motorcycle.

"I'll be fine. I'm a big girl."

The curtain in the living room window twitched. Someone was awake.

Gareth donned his helmet. "I'll pick you up between ten-thirty and eleven. A couple of places I want to show you. Get some sleep first, though."

Melissa started up the steps as the bike rumbled to life. She stopped at the top, turned and watched him leave.

Sucking in a deep breath, Melissa opened the front door and stepped over the threshold. Three pairs of eyes stared at her. "Where were you all night?" Danielle asked.

"You worried us to death, especially after yesterday," said Paul.

"Buddy was with her to keep her out of trouble," commented Gilles.

It was like she was a teenager again sneaking into the house in the early hours after being out with friends.

"The last time I looked, not one of you was my mother. Besides, I'll be twenty-nine at the end of the month. I don't need you lot running my life." She took off Gareth's jean jacket and clutched the coat to her chest. "If you must know, we took advantage of the tide being out last evening and walked out to the rock. After that, we went stargazing. The night sky was incredible. I guess we fell asleep."

"Sounds like the old 'we ran out of gas' excuse to me," Gilles teased.

Melissa took Buddy to their room before any one of them had a chance to speak. The temptation to slam the door was tempered by not wanting to frighten her dog. She unclipped the leash, then raised the denim garment to her nose and inhaled. Gareth's scent had faded. Soon it would be entirely gone. At least she was seeing him later so she could experience the real deal.

A soft rap on the door preceded Danielle's voice. "Can I come in?"

Not up for company, Danny's mainly, Melissa ignored the

knock. Her friend didn't go away. The rapping on the door became more persistent and louder until she entered the room.

"We need to talk. I need to apologize for earlier and the things I told you about Paul and me. Yes, we hung out together, but that was it. I guess I was just jealous of you." She paused, then continued. "I mean, you just broke up with one guy, and now you've got another one who's head over feet for you. If only I could be so lucky."

"You'll find someone."

"Not as long as I'm running this place, I won't. Percé isn't what you could consider a Mecca for single men. My social circle doesn't extend beyond grocery store employees, other business owners and guests. Any men who have come through here are husbands and fathers. I don't plan on ruining anyone's marriage or family."

Danielle's words about having a second guy in love with her finally sank in. Did Gareth feel that strongly about her? She was unsure if she loved him, although she felt something for him and anticipated seeing him. His kisses were electric. He wouldn't kiss her like that if he was leading her on, would he?

"We okay now?" Danielle asked, bringing her back to the present.

"Yes."

"Get some rest."

The door clicked shut behind Danny, and Melissa flopped on the mattress. In no time, she fell back to sleep. She dreamed of Gareth. Of waking up in his arms. Not under the stars on a blanket on the viewing platform but in a proper bed. Yesterday's ride on the back of his motorcycle, and he was taking her out again today. These thoughts and memories flashed through her mind like a movie trailer until a horrible one filled her with dread.

Gareth was back on active duty in a war-torn nation. Blood covered his entire body from wounds. His injured right arm had been blown off; his eyes clouded over. He was dead. Melissa sat bolt upright and tried to catch her breath. That vision was so real — more real than the others. She leapt off the bed, ran to the bathroom, and vomited.

Was it a premonition? Was Gareth going to die in an accident? She still trembled when he arrived at the agreed-upon time.

"Hey, what's wrong?" He drew her close and held her.

"I-I dreamt you died. Killed in action. It was awful," she cried.

He rubbed her back as he spoke. "I'm standing in front of you now, holding you in my arms, so I'm definitely not dead. Or if I am, so are you. I did my tour. I don't have to go back."

"I'm glad. I don't want to lose you that way."

"Ready to go? I have a couple of surprises for you."

Melissa dashed the tears away with the backs of her hands and blinked a few times to clear the others from her eyes. Why was what looked like his duffel bag fastened with bungee cords to the rear of the Norton? It wasn't there yesterday. She still wore the same clothing she had on when they went out the previous night. There was no time to change now. Besides, the more layers, the warmer she would be when they got moving.

She started towards the bike and was about to mount when she remembered he had to start the engine first. Gareth was not in any rush to get going, it seemed. He sat sideways on the seat, wearing a cheesy grin on his face.

"Did yesterday not teach you anything?"

"What do you mean?"

"I saw your hair flapping all over creation in my mirrors. Come here and let me fix it."

What was he going to do? She had layers on and could stuff her long brown mane inside the clothes like she did before, albeit too late.

Gareth turned her around, so her back was to him when she stood in front of him. He ran his fingers through her hair. She knew he was braiding it with the tugs from one side to the middle to the other.

"Got an elastic?"

Melissa fished one off her wrist and handed it to him.

"There. It's not perfect but won't be blown all over."

While Gareth started the engine, she buttoned the jean jacket, stuffed her smartphone in the pocket and put on her helmet.

Once mounted, she pushed down the right side footpeg and wrapped her arms around his waist in preparation for their ride. She'd been off and back on the motorcycle the day before a few times and was pleased with herself; she remembered everything.

Twelve

Chute de la Riviere Portage, near Percé, Québec

Where would Gareth take her today? Heavy traffic passed in both directions when they reached the highway. She peered over his shoulder. He had the right signal light on. That meant they were going north around the Gaspé once they got going.

They were only moving about ten minutes when Gareth slowed at the end of a gravel path leading towards the Gulf of St. Lawrence. The bumpy road made Melissa hold Gareth's waist tighter. After they rounded the sharp bend, a paved surface spread out before them. A small shelter covered a picnic table, and he brought the motorcycle to a stop beside it and killed the engine. Melissa dismounted. As she stood near the rear corner removing her helmet, Gareth engaged the kickstand.

The sun reflected off the river like thousands of diamonds, and she walked to the barrier made from vertical logs. Waves lapped at the packed sand making the setting peaceful. A few people strolled along the pavement in the distance. Some going away from them, while others approached. Gareth joined her. He came from behind and wrapped his arms around her waist. They stood in silence, mesmerized by the motion of the water before he took her by the hand, and they walked a short way to a set of stairs leading to the shore.

"How did you find this place?"

"Found it by accident on my way to Percé. I came from the other direction but couldn't go all the way down because of the rail line. The road ends on one side and starts again on the other. Had to turn around and go back to the highway. Tried again when I hit the first crossroad. Parked at the end next to the wall and walked the beach. I thought you might like to do it."

"Absolutely." Melissa placed her cheek on his upper arm. The heady combination of the brackish water, leather and his spicy body wash overwhelmed her. Her foot sank in the soft gravel, and she stumbled. Before she did any real damage, except to her pride, Gareth held her closely. She could happily spend twenty-four hours a day, every day, wrapped in his warm embrace.

At the next set of stairs, they returned to road level. An enormous, green porch swing hung from a wooden frame overlooking the river. Melissa led Gareth by the hand to it. "I love these," she said. "I wish Danny still had one at the guesthouse. They had one there when I was a kid. The patio table and chairs are there now."

"Nothing lasts forever," he replied flatly.

His tone frightened her. Did that mean that once he left Percé the following day, he would forget about her? She would be yesterday's news? She dropped on the swing and patted the seat. He joined her and, in moments, wrapped his arm around her shoulders. Maybe he was as upset about their time together coming to an end as she was? Melissa cuddled closer to him.

They remained in that position for about half an hour watching the water, the sun glinting off the surface, creating brilliant sparkles of light. Gareth broke the spell cast by the waves when he stood.

"Still more things I want to show you, so we best get a move on."

Reluctantly, Melissa rose. A motel, cabins, and a campground filled the neatly manicured land on the street's opposite side. Another swing was ahead of them in front of the green space dotted with red and white picnic tables and blue campsite markers.

They went back to the highway via the same narrow lane. After riding a short distance, they caught up with a pair of motorcyclists and rode along with them until Gareth slowed for a left turn.

Now, where was he taking her? The roadway was not overly wide, had no shoulders, but at least had a paved surface. A signpost stood in the brush not far from the intersection, but they were by before Melissa could read it. Birch and aspen trees lined both sides of the pavement. Gravel trails led off from one side or the other.

Melissa lifted the helmet's visor. The wind made her eyes water, but she didn't lower the acrylic shield. A hiking trail snaked off a parking area on their right where a lone van was parked. Black marks marred the road's surface from bikes or cars doing burnouts.

The road twisted and turned. They passed from sunshine to shade and back again. In one section, the bare ground on the left was red. Not quite Prince Edward Island red, but close. The back and forth movement combined with the constant vibrations erased her apprehension about being a passenger until the unthinkable happened. The asphalt ended, and they were on gravel when the back wheel skated out from under the bike.

Melissa squeezed her eyes shut and tightened her grip on Gareth's waist, sure they were going down. Her heartbeat pulsed through her eardrums and gums. They would die here in no man's land and never be found. Almost as quickly, he regained control.

Gareth parked next to a minivan. Melissa clambered off — no time for the proprieties of dismounting. She held her hands out in front of her. They still shook from the fright.

He stood before her with a cheesy ear-to-ear grin pasted on his face when she lifted her head.

"You scared me half to death! I thought for sure we were going down."

"You didn't like that little adrenaline rush?"

"No, I did not," she answered, fists at the ready to pound against his chest.

He thwarted her plan by grabbing her wrists and holding them tight.

He chuckled. The more Melissa struggled, the harder he laughed. The harder he laughed, the angrier she got.

"Calm yourself, will you? I got you here safely." Gareth busied himself, unbinding his duffel bag from the back of the Norton. When it was freed from its constraints, he placed it on the ground then, using the bungee cords, lashed his helmet to the motorcycle. "Here, give me yours."

She drew her arm back as if to pitch it at him.

"Not a good idea. Should we go down, you don't want a damaged helmet protecting your noggin." He reached out and took the headgear away from her.

"Look. If you must know, I've never had any desire to go on a motorcycle. Not after what I saw happen to Iain."

He never expected to hear that name. "What do you mean?"

"It was before we began dating. Actually, he was in the hospital when we started seeing each other. He owned one of those stupid motorcycles that looks like a racing bike and drove it like one down Water Street. A car ran the red light at the intersection outside the store. I witnessed the whole thing."

Gareth understood now why riding petrified her. The same as yesterday when they took the first corner fast. He stopped and placed his palms on her cheeks. Fear radiated from Melissa's eyes. He frightened her worse than he suspected. "I'd never intentionally do anything to hurt you. Not ever." He eased closer to her until their bodies touched.

A tear escaped her eye, and he brushed it away before lowering his mouth to hers and kissing her. He held her in that position until he felt the tension escape from her body. He saved her. He protected her, and now he scared her. If the bike had skidded and he couldn't regain control, he might have killed her. At the very least, she would have been injured. Gareth didn't care about himself, but he cared about Melissa.

"Where are we?" she finally asked.

Helmets secured to the bike's frame, he started away first. "Follow me." Gareth picked up the duffel bag, slung it over his right shoulder and wrapped his other arm around Melissa's shoulders.

They walked up the short hill to an uneven, root gnarled path. At this point, Gareth released Melissa so she could walk in front of him. The treacherous track was too narrow to continue beside one another, much as he preferred, but the wooden staircase leading down was nearby.

At first, there was not much to see as they descended. Soon that changed. Once beneath the canopy of leaves, the rugged landscape spread out before them. Water cascaded over the rocks into a blue-green pool. Melissa, a couple of stair treads ahead of him, stopped and took out her phone. She may have forgiven him by now because she was acting more like herself taking pictures — selfies and scenery.

The only problem with coming here was there were just as many steps to climb when they left. Descending was always kinder to Gareth's knees than ascending. At the bottom, he was able to draw next to Melissa again. Best of all, it was early enough in the season; they had the place to themselves.

Below the falls on one side was a steep rock face. Trees grew out of cracks and crevices, eliminating any access. Where they were, a pebbled shore stretched out. When he found the perfect place, he set the duffel bag on the ground and removed a blanket. Next, he pulled out a small cooler.

He purchased provisions before picking up Melissa. The small ice packs he used on his trip to Percé had been stored in the motel's freezer in the office until after his visit to the grocery store. Bottled water from the drink machine was already cold. Sandwiches on baguettes filled with ham, Swiss cheese, thinly sliced tomato, and shredded lettuce made up the picnic lunch.

"Come, get something to eat," he called to her.

"You brought all this? Wow!" Melissa lowered herself cross-legged to the blanket facing him.

She was beautiful. Gareth struggled to come to grips with his luck finding her. Not since his tour in Afghanistan finished had he spent any time with a woman. Thanks to his scars, both physical and psychological, he lacked the confidence to even attempt such a thing.

A shred of lettuce dangled on Melissa's lower lip, and he brushed the errant bit of vegetable away.

The two sat snuggled together, fingers entwined and watched the waterfalls until late in the afternoon. All too soon, the time came to make a start back up the hill to the Norton. Melissa folded the blanket while Gareth packed the cooler with the refuse from their meal. He'd dispose of it properly later.

Melissa trudged up the wooden steps ahead of Gareth to stretch out their time together. With her mind more on him than her surroundings, she didn't plant her foot firmly on the tread when she stepped on the next stair, and she stumbled.

Strong arms encircled her waist and kept her from falling. "Are you all right?"

She had a knack for making a fool of herself in his presence with her clumsiness. "Yeah. Not paying attention and kind of missed the step."

Hot, moist breath puffed on her neck followed the brush of Gareth's lips. His displays of affection sent butterflies flitting about in her stomach. She couldn't concentrate on anything other than his touch. If only he didn't have to go back; he was still attached to the military, so the choice was not his.

Still, it wasn't fair. Melissa knew she was selfish but didn't care. She only met Gareth four days ago and one of them she didn't see him at all so they'd only been together three. Three wonderful days. He introduced her to the freedom of motorcycling, and except for two incidents, laid her fears to rest. While she didn't think she'd ever buy her own, she was content with riding on the back of his.

Why, when she wished for time to slow down, did it seem to speed up? The cycle was constant. It only felt different — like when she was little, and Christmas took such a long time to arrive. The days and nights stretched forever. Now, when she wanted that, the seconds sped by at a breakneck pace.

All too soon, they arrived at the clearing above where Gareth parked his bike, and they could walk beside each other again. He wrapped his arm around her shoulder and pulled her tighter to him. In return, she cuddled closer and encircled his waist with her arms.

When they reached the motorcycle, Gareth removed the helmets from the back where he had secured them and deposited the duffel bag in that location, and bungee corded it to the bike's frame.

Melissa raised her helmet to put it on, but he rested his hand on hers and stopped her. He strode around the Norton's rear to where she stood and placed his palms on her cheeks, and kissed her — long and deep. She was not the only one who didn't want their time together to end so soon. Tomorrow. Too soon. The word tomorrow became his least favourite one in the dictionary.

If not for his moment at the motel, they would have had an extra day with each other, but that would have made leaving more complicated than it already was.

He held her tighter and committed every curve of her body to memory when the kiss ended. In a short time, that's all he would have. "I best get you back before they send out the hounds," he said, his voice husky.

"Only, if when we get back, you stay for a while."

Uncomfortable in social situations, Gareth wanted to refuse. Still, he couldn't deny himself more time with Melissa, even if the others would be there, too. "All right," he agreed.

Helmets donned, and the motorcycle started, Gareth waited for her to mount, and they set out. Her being so close to him made it difficult to concentrate, which might have been why the bike skated out on their way here. Focussed on the narrow road and the Norton's reactions to the gravel, he got them back to where the pavement began without any incidents.

After having spent so much time at the two places he took Melissa, it was after six o'clock by the time he pulled into the driveway at Fortin's Guesthouse.

Thirteen

Fortin's Guesthouse, Percé, Québec

"I talked Gareth into staying for supper. Hope it's all right," Melissa announced when they entered the living room.

"As long as he doesn't mind finger food."

"Fine with me," he said. "Mel and I ate lunch late, so we're not starving. At least I'm not. Are you?"

"No," she answered.

Buddy woke from his bed in front of the fireplace and raced to meet her. She bent over, and he jumped into her arms. "Hi, sweetie." She cuddled him close and scratched behind his ears. The little dog rested his head on her chest.

Gareth put his hand on Melissa's shoulder under Buddy's head.

"What's that delicious aroma?" Melissa inhaled deeply.

"Brie — two small ones baking in the oven along with a couple of baguettes." Danielle busied herself, retrieving plates and cutlery from the cupboards.

"I love hot Brie. How about you, Gareth?"

"Can't say as I've ever eaten it."

"You don't know what you're missing."

Melissa put Buddy on the floor, washed her hands and

helped Danielle with the meal preparations — not that there was a lot to do. She took the meats and hard cheeses out of the fridge, and arranged them on plates. Same with the carrot and celery sticks and cucumber slices. A dish of homemade French Onion Dip was in the refrigerator, too.

"I think we'll leave the cold things on the island where we can serve ourselves, then put the hot stuff on the table," said Danielle.

It made perfect sense, but there was too much food for them to eat in Melissa's mind, even with just this type of meal for supper. Well, perhaps everyone except Gilles. Danny's brother was a bottomless pit for as long as she had known him. Where he put everything he shovelled down his gullet, she didn't know. With the way the guy ate, he should have been the size of a house.

Gilles came into the kitchen from the back door as if on cue. That was the other thing; he could sniff out food miles away. Melissa smiled at him. "Paul not with you?"

"Making a phone call. He'll be in soon. Hey Gareth."

"Hi."

The savoury scent of the baking cheese filled the house. Gareth said he wasn't hungry, but the delicious aromas changed his mind. His mouth watered in anticipation of tasting the melted Brie.

"Quite the ride," Gilles stated.

"Thanks."

Paul temporarily interrupted Gareth's dreams of food when he entered the room and apologized for being late.

Soon, everyone had their cold plates filled and sat in the dining room. So far, Gareth was comfortable in everyone's presence. No panic attacks. Hopefully, it stayed that way.

Danielle carried the warmed cheeses in bright red baking dishes, one in each hand, and placed them at the table's ends before taking off the lids. Melissa brought over two baskets of sliced baguettes.

In the meantime, Gilles took over the seat at the head of

the maple-topped table. "I thought you'd want to sit next to Mel." He grabbed one of the spreaders and stabbed the hot Brie closest to him.

Gareth didn't object to not being in the same seat again. Here on the side with Melissa, he blended in rather than be on display.

"Norton motorcycles? Never heard of them," Gilles said.

"They're British. Made in North America for a while, but at least this model never really caught on." If they stuck to talking about his bike, he might be able to hold it together. Even if the conversation took a different direction, he would do his best not to experience a breakdown.

"How come you didn't ride it the first time you came here?" Danielle turned to him.

"Won't without proper boots. Mine got soaked jumping into the water after this one here." He patted Melissa's leg and smiled. "With only sandals, no bike."

"He's not sure about my high-tops," Melissa said. "But they were the best I had with me. My Doc Martens are back in Saint John."

"What year?" Paul tore the piece of bread he held and dipped it into a blob of melted Brie on his plate as he spoke.

"'74."

"Classic."

"Always owned motorcycles?" quizzed Gilles.

"No. This is the first."

"How long you had it?"

"About five years."

Melissa's hand rested on his thigh. She had his back. The subject was dicey. Gareth inhaled noisily, then took a mouthful of water.

"You did see action. I knew you did."

"No need to gloat, brother." Danielle shot her sibling a look.

"His best friend was killed in the war." Melissa jumped to his defence.

Maybe if he told everyone what he went through, it might be easier to deal with. "Our armoured vehicle, which should have been able to withstand a roadside bomb, didn't. I took shrapnel from my shoulder to my hand. Medics fixed me up best they could before they airlifted me to a military hospital in Germany. Spent time there after they filled me full of hardware to put my arm back together." He got through that much and not fallen to pieces, but he didn't mention Normand. Normand, who died without a mark on him.

A hush fell over the table.

"Are those scars on your hand part of the war wound?" Gilles pointed to the back of Gareth's injured extremity.

The guy was persistent and, at times, obnoxious.

"Yes. I had extensive physiotherapy, including shock treatment on the shoulder, which was hurt the worst. That was not a pleasant experience. Nothing seemed to be working — at least for any length of time. Finally, one of my specialists said I should get a motorcycle. Said the vibrations would help. Actually, he mentioned a Harley, but they were beyond my capabilities at that time. Maybe my next bike. And that, my friends, is how I ended up with Snortin' Norton out front."

"How much longer are you here in Percé?" Danielle asked.

"Not long. Leave in the morning. Due back at the base in Valcartier tomorrow night."

Melissa stood and walked away from the table. Gareth excused himself and followed her. "Let's go outside," he said and led her out the door and to the far end of the verandah.

"I wish you didn't have to leave," she said.

He drew her to him and held her. "I do, too, but the military is funny about you not being where you're supposed to be when you're supposed to be there."

She shivered, and he pulled her even closer.

Below the cliff, the tide receded. The black water was still except for the waves lapping at the shoreline. Oranges and reds filled the night sky. Tomorrow would be a good day for riding. The first sliver of the full moon peeked over the horizon. "Look." He positioned Melissa in front of him and encircled her waist with his arms.

The pinkish slice grew thicker and formed a crescent as it rose higher while they stood on the porch. Then it appeared to roll, and the craters on the moon's surface showed themselves over the water. The orb's familiar face became visible. The colour morphed from shades of pink to oranges.

Gareth leaned over and kissed Melissa's neck, then returned his focus to the rising moon. As it got higher, the colours faded, and it changed to white. Had she watched the spectacular sight? For all he knew, she could have had her eyes closed the entire time.

Melissa's body shuddered.

"Let's get you indoors. You're freezing."

She turned to face him and hugged him — her face pressed against his chest. He kissed the top of her head and moved her towards the door.

Back in the warmth, they resumed their meal in silence. The Brie remained warm inside the baking dish. Gareth enjoyed the gooey cheese's flavour, but not so much the rind's bitter taste.

"What do we want to do for the rest of the night?" asked Gilles. "Now the lovebirds have decided to grace us with their presence, again."

Gareth's ears grew hot, as did his face. He took a quick drink of water in the pretence he got a mouthful of jalapeño pepper in the cracker. As crazy as it sounded, after only knowing her for four days, he loved her. He would make sure she knew that before he left the following morning.

"Are the old board games still here?" asked Melissa.

"A couple of them. I've not thought about those things in ages," said Danielle.

Gilles groaned.

"I think Monopoly, Life and Clue are still here."

"Clue is fun. The other two take a long time to play. Why don't we do that?"

Melissa started to clear the table. Gareth joined her, and in no time, everything was put away.

Danielle returned with the game. "This brings back a lot of memories," she said. "You ever played, Gareth?"

"No. I was more baseball, hockey and BB guns when I was a kid."

"We amused ourselves with this for hours in the evenings when I came to Percé with Danielle in the summer. And when the storms knocked out the power, we carried on by candlelight."

"Not candles. By oil lamp. I still have it here."

"Why don't you light it, and we'll dim the rest of the lights. It will be like old times."

While Danielle left in search of the lantern, Melissa explained the rules to Gareth. "You'll have fun. I guarantee it."

"I won't play, but I'll put the who, where and how cards in the envelope," said Gilles. "You got to keep your eyes on these two," he nodded towards Danielle and Melissa, "they're sneaky."

Melissa scowled at him.

Cards dealt, characters chosen, and armaments laid out, they began. Melissa was Miss Scarlet as she was in the past. Paul took on the role of Professor Plum, and Danielle was Mrs. Peacock. Mr. Green, Mrs. White and Colonel Mustard remained for Gareth to select from. He didn't look like a female kind of character, so it left the two infamous males. In the end, given his background, he selected the military man.

Uproarious laughter ensued as the game progressed, and they whittled down the suspects, rooms and weapons.

"I want to make a suggestion," said Melissa.

Gilles took the packet from the middle of the board and held it close to his chest.

"I think it was Colonel Mustard with the lead pipe in the lounge."

Danielle challenged and revealed a card to Melissa.

Paul also showed one of his cards to her.

Mel added this information to her tally sheet, and they resumed.

On Gareth's turn, since his token was brought into the room, he suggested, "All right, Miss Scarlet, I think it was you here in this room, but with the revolver."

When it came time for Gareth's next turn, he said, "I'm

ready to make an accusation. Miss Scarlet in the billiard room with the knife."

Gilles opened the envelope and put the cards named by Gareth face up on the game board.

"How did you figure that out so quickly? There was still lots of missing information."

"Body language."

"From plastic tokens?"

"No from the people who are playing those characters." He smiled and winked at Melissa and reduced her to jelly.

It was almost midnight when they packed the board game away. Gareth won the first two games, Paul had one win to his credit, and Melissa rallied to take the fourth.

Mel followed Gareth to the door. "Do you want to take your helmet and jean jacket with you tonight?"

"No. You keep them here. I'll pick them up when I come to say my goodbyes in the morning." He leaned over and gave her a kiss on the cheek before going outside.

Fingertips resting on her face where he kissed her, Melissa walked out to the verandah. Gareth stood by the motorcycle and prepared to go. Tears coursed down her cheeks. She couldn't stop them, nor did she want to. He was leaving and save for a few minutes tomorrow when he returned for his belongings, she'd never see him again.

The steps in front of her creaked, and Gareth's arms pulled her into a hug. Her excuse with Iain was she was saving herself for her wedding night. Now, she didn't think she would ever get married. If she gave herself to Gareth, he might think she slept with every man she dated. No, she didn't want him to feel that way about her. No matter how much she craved it, she had to refrain.

His thumbs wiped away her tears, and he held her face in his palms and brushed his lips against hers. This kiss was different. His previous kisses were electrifying, but this one had an intensity that had not been there before. Was it because he didn't want to leave as much as she didn't want him to?

Melissa's fingertips curled into his shoulder blades as she clung to him. The kiss ended, and Gareth straightened up.

"See you tomorrow," he said and turned back towards the motorcycle.

With the engine started, and bike in gear, he headed down the long driveway. Melissa stayed outside until he was out of her sight.

Gareth pulled into the motel's parking lot and drove as quietly as possible with a Norton 850 Commando to the back of the building. Most of the rooms were in darkness, and he didn't want to wake anyone. He shut the bike off but didn't dismount when he reached the verandah outside his room. He enjoyed himself with the others to where he was comfortable talking about his time in the war. Pleased with himself, too, that he got through the evening without suffering a panic attack.

But he was still left with the problem of Melissa. She was not a problem per se, but it added to his anxiety levels when he thought of leaving her behind. Coming to Percé on two wheels meant he couldn't take her back with him. When he had his gear stowed on the back, there was barely room for him. But a second person and their bags and a dog? Impossible.

Slowly, he climbed off his ride and unbuckled his helmet as he walked up the few steps to his door. Tonight was going to be a long night.

Inside, he set his headgear on the desk, removed his leather jacket and tossed it on the chair, then flopped on the bed and stared at the ceiling.

Why didn't he tell Melissa how he felt about her before he left? Had he, it might have put her mind at rest. Tomorrow. He would tell her then. And if he didn't, shame on him.

Eventually, he fell into a restless sleep, but his dreams weren't about his time in the war. They were about his time with Melissa.

Fourteen

Motel Impérial, Percé, Québec

Gareth woke refreshed for the first time since before his tour of duty. Without stops or construction, it was a nine-hour ride back to Valcartier. He decided when he came to Percé, he'd return to the base via the south shore. That way, he could say he rode around the Gaspé, which also meant starting the trip for home sooner than later.

Showered, he gathered up his toiletries and medications from the bathroom. He grabbed his duffel bag and heaved it on the bed. When he unzipped the rucksack, the chiller bag and blanket from yesterday were still inside. Why didn't he stop at the motel before taking Melissa to Danielle's?

He opened the insulated container, removed the warm ice packs, and dumped the detritus from their picnic in the garbage. The gel-filled rectangular cubes should have been put back in the freezer in the reception area so they would be frozen and keep water cold on his trip. Sure, he could buy refrigerated drinks from the vending machine, but they wouldn't stay chilled.

Bag packed, he made an inspection of the room to ensure he left nothing behind. Satisfied he had collected all his belongings, Gareth slung the carryall over his shoulder, picked up the cooler and headgear, and walked out of the room.

Bungee cords secured everything to the bike. He ensured they were tight so he wouldn't lose anything in his travels. He still had a second helmet and jean jacket to stow.

Gareth started the motorcycle and drove to the front of the hotel to the office. Once checked out, he headed to Fortin's Guesthouse to say goodbye to everyone and retrieve the remainder of his gear. After that, the open road.

Melissa tossed and turned most of the night. The light outside her room had changed, meaning Gareth would arrive at any time. Unaware of the length of time it would take to drive from Percé to Valcartier, she hoped he could stay longer before he left.

The rumble of the Norton drifted through the air. She didn't want to hear that sound. According to the alarm clock in her room, it was going on a quarter after seven. Unsure how much time she had before Gareth arrived, Melissa tugged on a pair of leggings and yanked her hoodie over her head. At least she removed the remnants of her mascara the night before. Her eye makeup had run down her cheeks, mixed with tears.

She struggled into her wool work socks she liked to use as slippers because they were warm. Before she managed to pull both on, Buddy grabbed one and darted away with it. Silly dachsie. As verklempt as she was over Gareth's leaving, her dog's antics brought a smile to her face.

Once Melissa wrestled her sock away from the dog, she put it on and let him out to do his business. She followed but stayed on the verandah and sat on the top step. The wood was damp, and the seat of her pants got wet.

The noise from the motorcycle engine grew louder. Gareth was close to Rue Mont Joli, if not on it. All too soon, he rounded the corner of the house. This was the end.

Bike shut off, and on the kickstand, Gareth removed his helmet and dismounted. He sat next to Melissa, wrapped his left arm around her shoulders, and drew her to him. At first, she hesitated but within seconds gave in and pasted her body to his.

"You're going to get your butt wet," she said.

"As are you."

"Can't. Mine already is." The tears flowed again, and she turned her head away from him.

"I have something to tell you, and I'd rather say it to your face than the back of your head."

She started to turn back but only got as far as straight ahead. Hot, moist breath puffed near her ear.

"My, but you're stubborn. You're not making things easy for me, Melissa Scott. I love you."

Did she imagine hearing that, or had Gareth really said it?

The fingertips on his right hand touched her under her chin and guided her face towards his. Gareth's hand slid further up until her cheek rested in his palm.

"I love you," he said again. "Having to leave is tearing me up as much as it is you." His voice was husky.

Not her imagination. "I love you, too, Gareth. I wish you could stay."

"I know, but if I went AWOL when I finally did get back, I would be locked up."

"Jail? They'd put you behind bars for being late back."

"Absolutely."

That was unfair. Anything could happen to cause a delay getting back to the base — and especially something that might not be of Gareth's doing.

"Give me your phone."

"It's inside." Melissa stood. As she did, his fingers grazed hers. A jolt of electricity passed between them.

A few minutes later, she returned with her phone, the full-face helmet and his jean jacket. "Sorry, I took so long. I thought I left it on the nightstand, but it was still in the pocket of your coat." She relinquished her device. Had she removed the photo of the pill bottle? She intended to do that after she googled the medication. Mel tipped her head back and gazed skyward as if waiting for a miracle.

Gareth handed her phone to her along with his. "Here, put

your information in mine. My deets are already in yours."

Melissa sat back down beside him, pulled up the contacts and entered her cell number and email address.

In the meantime, Gareth gathered the other bits of gear and was stowing them.

By now, the others joined them outside. Buddy, now cradled in Melissa's arms, soothed her ragged emotions. She gave Gareth's smartphone back to him. "All in there," she said.

Handshakes shared with Gilles and Paul, and Danielle hugged, he turned to Melissa.

"You be a good Wienerschnitzel for your human," he said and scratched the dog behind the ears. "And you, behave yourself and don't cry too much. Your waterworks will fill the bay to the top of the cliff at low tide if you carry on like this."

It was just like Gareth to trivialize things. Melissa's breath hitched, and the tears she fought welled up in her eyes.

One more hug and electrifying kiss, and Gareth backed away and donned his aviator sunglasses.

"Take care of these two, eh, guys?" He gave his jean jacket to Melissa. "Keep it. Looks better on you anyway."

"You bet." All three responded in unison as they surrounded their friend.

Gareth put on his helmet, started the motorcycle and disappeared around the corner of the house.

All too soon, the drone of the Norton's engine faded completely.

Fifteen

Fortin's Guesthouse, Percé, Québec

Melissa tapped out a text on her phone. The tears she fought to contain before Gareth left flowed.

Be careful and let me know when you get home. Love you. x

He couldn't pick up her message while driving, but when he stopped, her missive would be waiting for him. With Gareth gone, nothing kept her in Percé. Mr. Peters promised her that her job would be there when she was ready to return. A week from Monday worked for her. The trains and buses between Saint John and Percé only available on certain days made travelling difficult.

Danielle placed her arm around Melissa's shoulders and walked her to the table and chairs in the corner of the verandah.

"Oh, Danny, what am I going to do?"

"Got it bad for him, don't you?"

"Yes."

"Could be worse. You could be pregnant."

Melissa fell hard for Gareth, knew the exact moment, but would they last? Rebound and long-distance, their relationship was doomed to fail. Best file these few days in the company of a broken soldier in her memories because they would be nothing more.

Ignoring Danielle's statement, Melissa said, "I'm going home on the first combination of buses and trains that works."

"You can stay here as long as you want," her friend answered and patted her knee.

"I don't want to abuse Mr. Peters' offer. He's been more than generous. I'll send him an email later. I doubt he's in the store today since it's Saturday. Usually, on the weekends, the assistant managers are on duty."

"If that's what you want."

Buddy scratched at her leg. She bent over and lifted the dog into her lap. "This one won't like being stuck in a cage for the better part of two days, but what are my options?"

Danielle petted the top of the dog's head. "We'll think of something."

Paul emerged from the house. "Sorry, Danny. I need to be back in Halifax on Monday. I'll be leaving tomorrow."

"Perfect! You can take Mel home. Save her the transit fare, and she and Buddy will be more comfortable in your car than on a bus or train."

He furrowed his brow. "Sure, why not. The company would be appreciated."

"Are you sure I'm not putting you out? I don't want to do that. I can make my way home myself."

"All I ask is be ready to leave by eight o'clock at the latest."

"I will." If Danielle's volunteering his services bothered him, he didn't let on. He might say something tomorrow along the drive. Until Paul needed to make the off-route trip into Saint John, it was the same road. If she could convince him to drop her off in Moncton at the train and bus station, she would make the rest of her way on her own and save him the detour.

Melissa went inside and composed the email to her boss. Still no response from Gareth, not even a progress report as to his whereabouts. Not wanting to bother him, she tried to push his absence out of her mind, but without success.

In her room, Mel laid out clothes for the next day and

packed the things she no longer needed. The less she had to do in the morning, the better.

Supper was a quiet affair. Melissa was occupied with thoughts of Gareth and his safety.

"Ten-ish when he got away?" Gilles glanced at the wall clock.

"Around that."

"North or South shore?"

"South. He said something about riding around the Gaspé."

"He'll be nine hours anyway without breaks. Probably closer to eleven if there's a lot of construction. I doubt he'll message you much before ten."

His words only made Melissa miss Gareth more. She didn't know if she could wait that long.

"How come you need to leave tomorrow, Paul?" Danielle asked.

"Important lawsuit came in. All hands are needed."

"That was the phone call you got?" Gilles turned to his friend. "Must be quite the case."

"Seems to be from the brief they emailed me. It's worked out for the best. Mel's leaving, too, so I'm taking her home."

Later that night, Melissa's iPhone vibrated on the nightstand. She snatched it off the surface and slid her finger over the screen.

Home now. All is fine. Miss and love you.

She tapped out a message in return.

Going home tomorrow. Paul needs to go back to Halifax, so I'm hitching a ride with him.

Before Gareth jumped to any conclusions, she typed another short line.

Danny voluntold him. Love you, too. Miss you. xx

Gareth lay back and stared at the ceiling. Less than twenty-four hours since he left Percé and Melissa, but it felt like a lifetime ago. He picked up his phone and scrolled through the pictures she copied to the device. If only he didn't have to leave her. Could have brought her and Buddy back to Valcartier with him. Damn the military and their stringent rules.

He lived in the unmarried quarters on the base, which was essentially a multi-storey apartment block. At least it was larger than a bachelor flats with everything but the bathroom in one area. When he finally returned from Afghanistan, someone had moved his possessions into this unit. All traces of Normand erased. Before their deployment, they shared a place. Now, Gareth rattled around alone. Even some of the other members of the Van Doos steered well clear of him. His attacking one believing the man was an insurgent didn't help.

Back on duty in the morning, if he didn't soon get some sleep, he'd miss roll call. Still, he couldn't rest. Every time he closed his eyes, the same vision flooded his mind. Melissa held by a member of the Taliban, Bowie knife at her throat. Was it because the next day, she'd be returning to Saint John where that loser she was engaged to lived? Was it because Paul Sutton was taking her home? After all, she said she had a crush on the man when they were both younger.

Gareth pulled the leather shaving kit bag out of his rucksack. He never used it for the purpose it was intended, but to carry all his drugs. He dry swallowed a couple of painkillers and a Sertraline capsule. Surely, once that combination took hold, he'd be in a dream-free slumber in no time.

He lay awake for hours, staring at the ceiling or rolling from one side to the other, punching his pillow into a more comfortable position.

Sixteen

CFB Valcartier, Québec

"Young, what's going on in there?" Loud pounding on the door echoed over his own battering.

"Someone's trapped. I need to save them," Gareth answered, not missing a stroke with the hammer as he pummelled the wall.

"It's the middle of the night. Get some sleep, will you? The rest of us sure want some."

Gareth continued his quest to rescue the person in danger.

"Help me," a female voice cried.

Not just any woman's voice but Melissa's. She was the one entombed in the cavity behind the drywall. He picked up his pace and ripped chunks of the gypsum board away from the studs. She wasn't there. Where did she go?

"Gareth, please," she called again.

This time she was in a different location. He rushed to that spot and pounded and pulled but again, no Melissa.

Eventually, the residents he woke gained access to his flat. One wrestled the hammer away from him, and another pinned him down on the bed until the Military Police arrived. Gareth struggled against the men. "I've got to save her," he argued.

"She's trapped."

"Who?"

"Melissa. Why won't you believe me? Someone stuck her in the wall. I was trying to free her."

A medic entered and injected him. He felt the prick of the needle followed by the rush of the medication. Within moments, he stopped struggling, and his body went limp.

Gareth woke in the infirmary the following morning with no memory of how he got there. His mind was fuzzy, no doubt caused by the pills he'd taken combined with whatever they shot him up with.

Gradually, things became less muddled, and the previous night's events were clear. He trashed his apartment. Tore chunks out of the walls. Why? That part remained a mystery.

As if things weren't already bad enough, Colonel Martin appeared in the door of his private room. He'd manage to avoid the stockade and a court-martial before but could he again? Gareth struggled to untangle himself from the bedding and come to attention to salute the senior officer.

"As you were, soldier."

Gareth sighed.

"I hear there was trouble in your apartment block last night. Your flat specifically."

"Yes, sir," he answered, bowing his head.

"I've been patient with you, Young. More than. We're all sorry about Normand Lévesque losing his life. Still, I'm afraid I can't let your anti-social behaviour wreak further havoc on my base."

"Yes, sir."

"We're having you transferred to a mental facility. See if maybe the specialists there can't straighten out that head of yours. After your release, you'll go to the transition unit where you'll receive retraining for another post in the military or in civilian life." The colonel stood and exited the room, pausing to speak with someone in the corridor.

Psychiatric ward. Gareth hit rock bottom with that news.

No matter how supportive Melissa was back in Percé, he couldn't tell her. He had to sort himself out, regardless of how daunting the task.

Seventeen

Carruthers residence, Saint John, New Brunswick

Six months later ...

Ed Carruthers sat at the kitchen table with his coffee and newspaper. Not long after he accepted the warden position at the Saint John Regional Correctional Facility, something had been off in his marriage. They lived in a small segregated section of the prison when they first moved in. However, when word came of a new subdivision near work, he and his wife bought in before the local dignitaries broke ground.

Now, as he sipped his dark roast and skimmed over the headlines, his mind wandered. Yvonne didn't want for anything. He was an excellent provider and spoiled her with new clothes, trips, jewellery, her Mercedes, and an incredible cleaning woman who came once a week. What baffled him was the day before the housecleaner's arrival, Mrs. Carruthers cleaned the house from top to bottom. Her excuse being the domestic couldn't come into a mess. He never saw anything that constituted that.

The stress of the job took its toll on him. Once slim and

reasonably fit, he was soft, pudgy and overweight. His once black hair, what remained, was practically white.

Yvonne aged much better than he, attended the gym regularly. Owned enough beauty products — moisturizers, sculpting creams, and others he had no clue what she used them for — she could start her own spa. She even dyed her long hair blonde. He loved her and could forgive any transgressions, but he needed to hear it from her. After months of speculation, he would confront her today.

His wife soon joined him at the table dressed in a long, white satin robe and matching pyjama pants. Barefoot as usual indoors, her bright orange-red nail polish on her toes matched that on her well-shaped fingernails. She did put in the effort, but was it for him or someone else?

"Have you taken your blood pressure pills yet, Ed?"

The man huffed out a sigh.

"You'll die of a stroke or a heart attack if you don't start taking proper care of yourself." Yvonne retrieved the pill bottle from the counter by the sink and poured him a glass of water.

"You'd like that, wouldn't you."

"What do you mean by that?"

"Nothing."

He almost brought up his suspicions, but the doorbell chimed, putting an end to the discussion. Ed left the room and went to see who was at his front door on a Sunday morning. He opened it to a tall, thin uniformed police officer with reddish-blonde hair. His name tag read R. Robertson.

"Sorry to bother you so early, Warden, but one of your men was in a life-threatening motor vehicle collision."

"You best come in then."

He ushered the policeman to the kitchen. "Coffee?"

"No, thank you."

"So one of my men, you say."

"Yes." The cop pulled out a chair and sat. "He was in uniform, so I'm guessing he was on his way to work."

"Do we know who he is?"

"Yes. Found the man's ID badge in the vehicle. An Iain Mallory. Located the lad's phone, too."

Yvonne choked on her mouthful of coffee. It couldn't be, not her Iain.

"Are you all right, Mrs. Carruthers? You're a bit pale."

"Yes, yes. I'm fine." Far from it, but she had already attracted enough attention. "What about Iain Mallory?"

"I'm afraid things aren't looking promising, which is why I'm here. I need his next of kin information."

"That severe?" Ed asked.

"Yes. A train T-boned Mr. Mallory's car at the level crossing on Bayside Drive. Witnesses say the barriers and lights were working at the time. Our guess is, he was running late for work and didn't or couldn't stop in time. The small Honda was no match for the locomotive. The impact tore the car in half."

The room swam in front of Yvonne. She slid off the chair and collapsed on the floor in a faint. Visions of her lover battered, bruised and bloody flashed through her unconscious mind. It couldn't be happening. It couldn't be real. It had to be someone else. Her husband and a concerned police officer stood over her when her eyes fluttered open.

The men helped her back on the seat. The expression on Ed's face told her she had been found out. Things had been strained between them for a long time, and she figured he knew about her affair and now, thanks to her not keeping her emotions in check, had handed him all the proof he needed. By all accounts, Iain would die, so she couldn't go to him when Ed packed her bags and kicked her out. What a mess.

"Come with me. I keep a file in the study in case of emergencies. Never thought a car accident would be the cause. Always figured it would be something at the facility," the warden said.

Ed gave her one last disdainful glare before leaving the room.

When Yvonne first started her fling with Iain, it was fresh, exciting, dangerous. That was the thrill. They were caught just before he broke up with her by his fiancée, no less. She was stupid to think they would be safe in one or the other's homes, but Iain assured her they would be. Melissa wouldn't be anywhere near the condo because he was scheduled to work that day.

Hot tears scorched her cheeks. She dashed to her bedroom and slammed the door before throwing herself across the bed and sobbing.

"Is your wife going to be all right?"

"She'll be fine. It might be the wake-up call she needs. Now, let's find that information." Warden Carruthers took a key out of the top desk drawer and unlocked his filing cabinet. "I keep a list here because you never know."

He pulled the file out and opened the folder. "Mallory, Mallory, Mallory," he muttered as he ran his finger down the listing of employees sorted by their surnames. "Ah, here we go. Melissa Scott." He turned the page so the officer could take down her contact details. "You said you found his phone as well? Given he's a young person, he likely has all that in it."

"You're probably right. Thanks for your help and give my regards to your wife."

Ed escorted the policeman outside and stood there watching while the man climbed into his cruiser. After closing the door, he leaned against it. Until his wife's reaction to the news, the warden never would have imagined Iain Mallory would be the one. He, a hardworking, trustworthy young man. Now, he knew differently; it was time to confront Yvonne.

Bursting into her bedroom — they slept in separate rooms for quite some time because of his snoring and later his CPAP machine. She used that as her excuse. He strode to the bed, grabbed her by the arm and hauled her into a sitting position. "I think it's time we had a little chat, don't you? Then, we're getting dressed and going to the hospital to show our support for my employee, or should I call him your lover."

"I despise you, Ed Carruthers," she spat.

"Maybe so, but you don't hate all the things I give you," he gloated. "How long have you and Iain been carrying on behind my back?"

"What difference does it make? It's over. Been finished for a long time."

"Your reaction says otherwise." He folded his arms across his chest, not believing a word his wife said.

"Get out."

He didn't budge.

"Get out of my room."

Ed held his ground.

"You say we're going to Saint John Regional. Then leave me alone so I can shower and dress."

"We're still going to talk about this."

Melissa's iPhone rang. She plucked the device off the nightstand next to her bed and glanced at the display. Iain. She immediately slid her thumb over the screen, disconnecting the call. Months had passed since he last bothered her. Why suddenly now? It rang again. Same number. Again she disconnected. When it happened a third time, she accepted. "I don't want anything more to do with you, Iain Mallory. Now get out of my life." After she shouted that, she hung up.

The annoying ringtone started again, tempting Melissa to throw the thing across the room, but she answered it instead. "What part of get out of my life don't you understand?"

"Wait, don't hang up."

That wasn't Iain's voice.

"I'm Constable Robertson with the Saint John Police Force."

Why was a cop phoning her, and more importantly, why from Iain's phone?

"Can I come to see you? I must speak with you."

"Sure."

"I'll be there in about fifteen minutes." The call disconnected.

She didn't give him her address. How would he find her? With no time to shower, she washed her face, brushed her teeth, put on deodorant and got dressed. A knock sounded on her door as she was brushing her hair.

Melissa peered through the peephole then pulled the door open.

"You might want to sit down," he said and nodded to her sofa.

Buddy came tearing out from the bedroom, barking. "Quiet you," she said and picked the dachshund up to settle him.

The cop walked closer and squatted in front of her. A shock of Constable Robertson's strawberry blonde hair fell on his forehead, and he brushed it back. "I have bad news, I'm afraid. Iain Mallory was in a near-fatal motor vehicle collision. He listed you as his next of kin on his employment documents."

They hadn't been together since late May. Why didn't he update his information? Then it hit her. He grew up in the foster care system and had no one other than her.

"Wha-what happened?"

The officer repeated the cause of the accident he provided to the warden earlier. "We should leave for the hospital as soon as possible. I'll drive you."

Melissa grabbed her purse and iPhone then motioned to the policeman to go out first so that the dog didn't escape. She and Buddy had an exit routine that worked well. A doggie treat sent skidding across the floor, which the dachshund happily chased. Those few moments of running and eating gave her plenty of time to grab a coat from the hook and duck out the door.

Mind reeling from the news, she blindly snatched the garment. Not until she was in the hall did she realize she grabbed Gareth's jean jacket that he left with her when he went back to Valcartier after their brief time together in Percé.

The cruiser sped through the quiet Sunday morning streets of Saint John. Melissa leapt out of the passenger seat when the car came to a stop outside the emergency department. Constable Robertson guided her by the elbow through the busy seating area to the triage nurse.

"We're here about Iain Mallory," he said.

Without looking up, the woman shuffled some papers on her desk, typed something on her computer. "In surgery. You can go through to the surgical suite waiting room."

"Where is that?" Melissa whispered.

"I'll take you," the cop said.

The designated space didn't amount to much — just a bunch of chairs lined up along the walls. A set of double doors signposted authorized personnel only at the end. Melissa dropped into one, thankful for the upholstered seat and back rather than the usual hard plastic.

"Is there anyone I can phone for you? Anything you need before I leave?"

"No, thank you."

"If you do, call me here." He handed her a business card with his badge number written on the back.

Tears welled up in Melissa's eyes. What had Iain been thinking running through the railway barriers? It was insane to try to beat a train. She pulled out her phone. The battery was at less than thirty percent, and the device would have to be charged. She scanned the room and found an outlet on the opposite side, farther down from where she sat.

Melissa plugged in the extra charger she carried with her and attached the other end of the cable to her iPhone. She searched for Danielle in her text messages and tapped one out to her.

Life is unfair.

A few moments later, a response came through.

What's wrong?

Melissa took a deep breath. At this point, what was right?

Iain's been in a terrible car accident. I'm at the hospital now.

She tipped her head back to keep her tears from spilling down her cheeks.

Iain? Don't you mean Gareth? Danielle texted.

Her phone rang before Melissa had a chance to type her reply. Danny's information filled the display.

"What's going on? You've confused me."

"Iain was in an accident on his way to work this morning. They don't think he's going to live."

"Oh, sweetie. This might sound crass, but what does it have to do with you?"

"I'm listed as his next of kin."

"Oh. Is there anything I can do?"

"No, I'll be fine once I'm over the shock."

A man and woman entered the room arguing. Melissa couldn't figure out what they were saying other than the woman was upset, and the man was angry. The pair sat across the corridor from her, and although they still bickered, they lowered their voices so she couldn't hear.

When she finally worked up the nerve to find out who these people were, it was the face of the woman she caught with Iain. Melissa ducked her head. It had to be her imagination. She needed to calm down. If only Gareth were here with her. He would know what to do. What to say.

Melissa cast her eyes towards the double doors. It was going to be a long day.

Footsteps grew closer, and stopped in front of her chair. "You're Melissa Scott, aren't you?" the man asked.

"Yes. Why?"

"I thought so. I'm Ed Carruthers, the warden at the correctional facility where Iain worked … I mean works."

The man was older, probably in his early sixties, with thinning grey hair and balding, likely about the same age her father would be if he were still alive.

"When the young constable came to the house this morning looking for Iain's next of kin, I saw your picture on his phone."

"Do you have it?"

"No, the police do. I'm sure it will be released to you soon."

Speaking with her, his voice was soft and caring, unlike when the two blew into the room.

"Have you met my wife, Yvonne?"

Melissa looked at the woman then shook her head.

"I'm going to get us a coffee. Can I bring something back for you?"

"Yes, please. You're kind to offer."

Mr. Carruthers disappeared around a corner.

"Thank you for saying we've never met."

"I didn't do it for you." Melissa stood and took a couple of steps forward. "I know exactly who you are and what you and Iain got up to when you were with him. I caught the pair of you in bed, remember?" Mel's voice rose with each word.

Yvonne squirmed in her seat, and Melissa turned around, smiling. It looked good on the woman.

The latch on the doors at the end of the corridor clicked. A doctor in scrubs, rubber boots and cap approached. "You're here for Iain Mallory?"

"Yes," both women answered in unison.

"Which one of you is his next of kin?" He turned to Yvonne.

"I am," said Melissa.

"Please, sit."

The surgeon sat beside her when Mel returned to her chair. He took her hands in his gently. "I'm sorry, but he didn't make it. His injuries were too severe."

A strangled sob escaped Melissa's lips.

Yvonne howled.

The woman was such a drama queen. What had Iain ever seen in her? Besides the obvious. He wanted, and she was willing to give.

"C-can I see him?" Melissa asked.

"Not yet. There are a few more formalities to go through first before the body is released to the funeral director."

Funeral. She never planned one in her life. Didn't even help out when her father died. Supposedly, it had all been pre-planned. Was Iain that organized?

Mr. Carruthers returned, clutching three cups of vending machine coffee. "What's going on?"

"He's dead," wailed his wife.

Melissa wanted to slap the woman. Do anything to shut her up. All she was to Iain was a roll in the hay. Wild oats sown while she had known Iain for the better part of five years. They got engaged on New Year's Day of this year and planned on marrying the following January 1st. Mel broke it off before it could happen. If he couldn't be trusted before they married, then how could he be afterwards?

"Yvonne, you're making a fool of yourself," her husband snapped, and just as quickly, he turned to Melissa and said, "Don't you worry about a thing. The wife and I will take care of the arrangements. Do you know if he had a preference as to which funeral home he wanted? If he had a will?"

She shook her head. "You're very kind. Iain has a strongbox back at our condo. I assume everything would be in it." Referring to her dead fiancé in the present tense was surreal.

"Let me give you my card. If you need anything, don't hesitate to call me. This is my work number, and this ...," Mr. Carruthers jotted something on the reverse, "is my cell phone. You can reach me on either."

"Take as much time as you require," said the surgeon. "There's no rush."

"Can we offer you a ride home?"

The last place Melissa wanted to be was in a car with Yvonne, the drama queen, Carruthers. She needed this time to be on her own to take in the enormity of the situation. She wanted to talk to Gareth.

Eighteen

Saint John Regional Hospital, Saint John, New Brunswick

The walk to the condo from the hospital was over an hour. That was fine with Melissa. That much more time to be on her own and try to reconcile herself with the situation. Even the vibrant fall colours failed to soothe her. Autumn was one of her favourite times of the year, but it was destroyed in one day. The sun was blindingly bright. Was that why Iain ran the barriers? Was he blinded and didn't see they were down?

Most of the walk was on the shoulder of the road. There were no sidewalks until much closer to the heart of the city. Even though Melissa still had a long hike to her house, it didn't seem as bad because there were more than trees, rock cuts and guardrails. She would stop at her apartment first, get Buddy and take him for a walk.

The green overhead Trans-Canada Highway signs were a welcome sight. Her home was close to the motorway. Sometimes at night, the traffic noise drifted in through her open windows. Melissa breathed a sigh of relief when she arrived at the corner of Garden and Coburg Streets. Her house was in sight.

Inside, she poured a glass of water then flopped on the sofa. Melissa pulled out her iPhone and scrolled through the pictures. Not one of Iain remained. She deleted everyone he appeared in when she hitched a ride with Paul back to Saint John. Now, she regretted her actions. With her being Iain's next of kin, undoubtedly, his phone and his personal effects would be returned to her? The tears flowed again.

Melissa's fingers hovered over Gareth's name in her contact list. She needed to speak to him but hesitated because he might not understand her grief. Instead, she opened the text messaging app and sent a short, two-word one to Danielle.

He's dead.

Nothing she could say or do would bring Iain back. She still hadn't had the opportunity to say goodbye — too many things to do other than dwell on the past. First, Melissa ensured she still possessed the key to the condo. Without it, she couldn't get in and check the strongbox for documents.

After the month-long stay in the mental facility, Gareth felt more like his pre-Afghanistan self. Group therapy with other military members who, like him, suffered from PTSD and one-on-one counselling with a psychotherapist, something he didn't receive previously.

When he returned from seeing action, the first round of treatment didn't help much, if at all. Mostly, the medics pushed pills on him. This time, he connected with the specialist. There were still drugs, but the doctors monitored his reactions to the medications and the dosages.

Gareth still had good days and bad ones. The bad occurred when his arm played up or on the anniversaries of traumatic events and sometimes lasted for weeks. He put his motorcycle in storage before being hospitalized. A month without riding caused his shoulder to stiffen and ache worse than usual.

At least the Canadian forces gave him twenty-four hours to tidy up his affairs. That was also the last time he spoke with Melissa. He'd not made contact with her since. Never mentioned what was going on. He couldn't tell her he was committed to the nuthouse. But the end of that time drew nearer every day.

During one of his personal sessions, the possibility of Gareth obtaining a service dog came up. More specifically, an emotional support dog. He always liked dogs, even Melissa's, who snapped at him the first time he met the animal.

Later today, his psychotherapist was taking him to see a group of golden retrievers that were being trained as ESDs. He might come home with one, or choose the one he wanted, or decide it wasn't for him.

Next up, come to terms with the transition unit. Retraining. All Gareth knew was the army. He and Normand enlisted as soon as they were old enough.

Today would be the day he phoned Melissa. He was sure of that, if not anything else in his life.

Rested and refreshed, Melissa clipped the lead to Buddy's collar, and they set out. Tree-lined grass boulevards lined the street until they made it into the commercial area of the city. Construction, road and buildings, created blockages or places, forcing her to walk on the pavement because the sidewalks weren't accessible. When she arrived in these sections, she carried Buddy. Melissa hoped she was big enough for drivers to see, but her dog certainly was not.

The city switched from commercial to mixed residential with convenience stores, apartment complexes and office blocks. None of the properties had a front yard. Buildings stood next to the sidewalk; some were tagged with graffiti.

Once past the construction zones, she set him down so he could walk. Buddy was the cliché dog. He stopped and sniffed every pole and tree before peeing on them. A journey that would generally take Melissa fifteen to twenty minutes stretched to over half an hour. It would have been longer, but she won the battle of wills and decided when it was time to move on.

At the foot of the condo's stairs, she picked up the dachshund and sighed. This was going to be an extremely unpleasant task. Melissa trudged up the six steps to the landing, unlocked the door and crept in. The rooms were dark, and she reached for the light switch.

Where had she seen the fireproof box? Leash unclipped, she put the dog down, and started for the stairs, then turned and went to the kitchen instead. Systematically, she went through the cupboards but didn't find what she was looking for. Next, Melissa opened the fridge. Milk, orange juice, mustard, mayonnaise and cold cuts. In the freezer section, bread. Iain's refrigerator was bare compared to hers.

Neither the living room nor dining room held the elusive safe. It had to be upstairs in one of the two bedrooms. Melissa hoped Iain didn't store it in the room where she caught him red-handed with his lover.

As she climbed the steps, memories of that fateful day rushed back — even the sounds from their lovemaking. Melissa covered her ears to drown out the noise but to no avail. The racket came from within her mind, and no external blocking would muffle the sound.

The second bedroom off to the right of the landing revealed nothing. Iain's uniforms hung in the closet. What should she do with them? The drawers of the dresser were empty, as were those in the nightstands.

Melissa had no choice but to check the master bedroom. When she pushed the door open, a wave of nausea hit her. Bile rose in her throat, and Mel clapped her hand over her mouth and dashed to the bathroom. Somehow she managed not to vomit. She wouldn't spend one minute longer than necessary in here. She opened the closet's bifold doors, and there above the clothes rail with the key dangling from a tie strap on the handle sat the fireproof safe. Surprised by its weight, when she snatched the box down, Melissa almost dropped it.

Too heavy to take back to her apartment, she had to stay here and go through its contents, much to her chagrin. She plodded back down the stairs and laid the container on the dining room table. Her hand shook as she tried to unlock it. Did Iain keep other secrets from her? With trepidation, she raised the top.

Letters and various documents were crammed inside. Tucked into one corner sat a box embossed with the crest of a jewellery store. Melissa took it out and removed the lid. Her engagement ring stared back from within the velvet lining. Apparently, Iain hoped they might reconcile. Melissa went back to the paperwork. A life insurance policy naming her beneficiary. Deed to the property in both his and her names. In her grief and confusion, she forgot they had bought the place together. It seemed a lifetime ago. Mortgage insurance policy. The condominium would be fully paid for.

Carbon copies of confidentiality agreements from the Correctional Facility were among the papers. Presumably, the jail retained the originals. An envelope from a funeral home was next on the pile. At least she knew where to have his body released. Finally, she discovered another bearing the name of a local law firm. She took the document out and unfolded it. Iain's will. He left everything to her.

Her iPhone vibrated. Gareth's name filled the display. Could she deal with him on top of everything else? Melissa sighed and slid her finger across the screen. "Hiya," she said, trying to sound cheerful.

"What's wrong?"

"Nothing." After a long pause at both ends, she blurted out, "Iain's dead." Melissa managed to hold it together as long as possible before she sobbed down the phone. "I don't know what to do."

"What do you mean he's dead?"

"Just what I said. Iain was in an accident on his way to work this morning, and he died later in the hospital."

When it came to Iain's name, Gareth couldn't be sympathetic. Not after what he did to Melissa earlier in the year. "I thought you'd be jumping for joy to have him out of your life." Those words slipped off the end of his tongue with ease, and now he couldn't take them back. "I didn't mean that." But he did. With how torn up Melissa was when Iain showed up in Percé, he couldn't help but mean what he said.

"I'm overwhelmed at the moment. Where am I supposed to start? I'm the sole beneficiary and executor of his estate. I'm way out of my depth."

"What do you want me to do?" He meant his words in the best of terms, asking if he could assist her, but his tone said the opposite.

"I knew better than to tell you. You've been jealous of Iain and what I had with him since we first met."

"Jealous? I don't think so; the guy was a jerk. He didn't deserve you. He got what was coming to him."

"He what?" Melissa couldn't believe what Gareth said. "Well, if that's the way you feel, goodbye," she yelled into the phone before disconnecting and slamming the device down on the wooden surface. Until now, Melissa thought Gareth was different. She was so wrong. Men. Why did she bother to get involved with them?

Melissa buried her face in her arms and wept. The man was cold and callous, yet he seemed so warm and caring in the beginning. Their time together in Percé, while too short, was fabulous. He was fun to be with. He made her laugh. She sure knew how to pick them. Maybe she should have turned and run after the incident in his motel room. If not, then, after finding out he was on anti-depressants.

She reached into her pocket and pulled out the business card the policeman had given her. Flipped over his credentials and took in his badge number on the back. Not the one she wanted. Iain's boss gave her one, too. Where did she put it? Melissa dug around in all her pockets and found the one from the warden. There was no sense calling him at the jail because being Sunday, he'd probably be at his house. She laid his card face down, picked up her iPhone and called the number he gave her.

"Hi, it's Melissa Scott. I met you at the hospital a while ago," she said when the call connected.

"How are you bearing up?"

"Not well, but I'll manage. I'm at Iain's going through his

papers. I'm so confused."

"Is there something I can help you with?"

"Yes. No. I'm not sure."

"Give me the address."

Melissa rattled off the location and added, "Across the street from the Marco Polo Terminal."

"Now that you say that, I know exactly where you are. I'll be with you in half an hour at the most."

Call completed, she leaned back in the chair. Buddy made himself comfortable on the arm of the sofa closest to the front window. When Mr. Carruthers arrived, the dog's barking would announce it long before the doorbell rang.

She should offer the man a coffee at the very least, so Melissa wandered into the kitchen. A coffeemaker sat on the counter. Now to find the rest of the things she would need. She had to make sure the milk in the fridge was fit to drink before that. She opened the carton, but all she could smell was the waxed cardboard. The real test would be if it curdled in the hot brew. She would make herself a cup as soon as the appliance finished dripping.

Happy it didn't sour when she poured it into her mug, Melissa went back to the dining room and the spread-out stack of papers. Where to start? She pulled the hair elastic off her wrist and tied her hair in a ponytail. Suddenly, the memory returned of Gareth braiding it before he took her out on his motorcycle the second day. She needed to call him and apologize for losing it on him.

Currently, her emotions were still too raw and rather than say something wrong, she decided to wait for at least twenty-four hours — give herself time to adjust to the day's events.

As predicted, Buddy barked and ran to the front door announcing the man's arrival. Melissa pushed him away with her foot, but the dachshund persisted.

"You'll have to excuse Buddy. He's a bit excited."

"Is this Iain's wiener dog?"

"No, mine."

Mr. Carruthers nodded.

Melissa showed him to the dining room and the paper-strewn table. "Can I get you a coffee? I just made a pot."

"Thank you. Black, two sugars, if it's not too much trouble." The man took the chair previously occupied by her. "Working in corrections, we've always advised our people to have their affairs in order. Something terrible could happen at any moment. I'm glad to see Iain heeded the advice."

She placed his drink in front of him and sat opposite the man. "But where do I start?"

"I'll make the call to Brenan's for you, and they'll pick up Iain's remains at the hospital. By the looks of this, he pre-arranged everything. No visitation, and he wanted to be cremated. They'll also issue you as many copies as you'll require of their certificates of death. You'll need to provide a copy to his life insurance carrier, the mortgage insurance holder, among other things."

"But what about this?" Melissa scrabbled through the documents covering the table for the will. "I'm so lost."

Mr. Carruthers patted the back of her hand and took the papers from her. "Tomorrow, we'll make an appointment with his lawyer. Assuming no one comes out of the shadows with a claim to his estate, it should be settled in no time."

"Thank you for this. I wouldn't know where to start."

"The government requires you to complete a year-end tax return. I'll look after that since Iain worked for me."

Melissa sipped her coffee, grateful someone was with her who knew what to do. The warden excused himself and went to the foyer. He spoke to someone, but the person's identity on the other end of the phone remained unknown. She hoped he was talking to the funeral home. The sooner the nightmare was over, the happier she'd be.

The man returned a few moments later. "I think we've done as much as we can for one day. You shouldn't leave these papers here. They'd be safer at your place. Shall we gather this up, and then I'll give you two a ride home?"

"Thank you." Melissa gathered the papers and stuffed them back in the strongbox. She clipped Buddy's leash to his collar, and they started for the front door. Mr. Carruthers carried the safe.

"Wait a sec. Can't leave yet." She bolted for the kitchen to shut off the coffeemaker and collected their mugs from the dining room table. Gathering the beakers, she dumped the dregs down the sink, rinsed them and set them in the dish rack. She did the same with the carafe and tossed the grounds in the garbage. She had to come back later in the week to put out the trash.

By the time she reached the foyer, the warden had Buddy loaded into the car. Melissa closed the door behind her and ensured it locked. When she and Iain bought the condo together, she was filled with hope and anticipation. Now, the sadness of what once might have been, but now never would be enveloped her.

Gareth bent forward, rubbed his forehead with his fingers and regretted having been so snarky. The first time he'd spoken to her in a month, and he blew it. He needed to contact Melissa and apologize. He looked up her number and pressed the green button. Not surprisingly, she declined. He tried again but received the identical result. A text — she might not read the message, but the chances of her looking at it were greater than accepting his call.

Maybe once she mellowed, she would realize he didn't intend it the way he said. Iain caused her enough grief when he was alive, and now he continued from the afterlife.

I'm sorry. I didn't mean it the way it came out. I know you had a past with Iain, and I can't take that away from you. I care about you.

He read over his words a few times and hit send. Only time would tell if she would respond. Damn his attitude. If only he could turn back the clock. Go back to their time together in Percé. Since his return from Afghanistan, it was the best time he ever had.

Nineteen

Melissa's apartment, Coburg Street, Saint John, New Brunswick

Melissa's phone vibrated. She picked it up out of habit. Gareth again. This time he sent her a text. She turned off the screen and laid it back in her lap.

"Where can I drop you?" Mr. Carruthers asked.

His voice snapped her back to the present. "Coburg Street." For some odd reason divulging her complete address didn't seem appropriate. "At the intersection with Peters." If the man couldn't find her house with that much description, he wouldn't find the place with the house number either.

She rested her head on the headrest and exhaled. Traffic and construction caused numerous delays, but finally, he pulled the car to a stop around the corner from her home.

"Here you are. Do you need me to give you a hand into your house?"

"No, thank you. I'll be fine. Thanks for all your help this afternoon."

"I didn't do much, if anything."

"You helped me feel less overwhelmed, and for that, I'm extremely grateful." Melissa climbed out of the passenger seat and collected Buddy and the strongbox from the back. "Bye, I appreciate everything," she said as she closed the doors with her hip and waited for him to drive away.

Now, the fact Iain cheated on her earlier in the year was of little consequence. What mattered most, he died. She didn't say goodbye. With no visitation, she probably wouldn't be able to. She needed to phone the funeral home. Hurt and angry at Iain's betrayal, Melissa still loved him. Trusted him? Never. He shattered their marriage and her dreams of spending their lives together into thousands of pieces. Her pain was as if one of those shards pierced her heart. Her breath hitched.

By the time Melissa reached the top floor of the building, her arm ached from the weight of the fireproof box. Inside her apartment, she sat the safe on the island, unsure where to store the blasted thing. She couldn't stand the sight of it because it reminded her of him, and that brought back the memories of catching him and Yvonne in bed.

Overcome with guilt, Melissa went into her room and threw herself on the bed and cried. She was not the one who had done wrong. What made her remorseful? Was she angry with Gareth and his reaction to Iain's death? It was too much to bear.

She fell into a restless sleep filled with bizarre dreams — her wedding day, January 1, 2018. Dressed in her white gown with the matching fur-trimmed, hooded winter midi-length coat next to her brother, Roger, who walked her down the aisle.

Iain waited at the altar. But instead of Iain, his corpse took his place, and she was covered in blood. Gareth stood there as the best man. He pushed the groom over, and Iain's body shattered. All of a sudden, she was the only live person in the room. Everyone else transformed into mannequins, including wedding guests.

Panic-stricken, Melissa shot off the mattress. Her eyes darted back and forth, taking in her surroundings. She was in her bedroom in *her* apartment, not in a chapel where every living being morphed into a dummy. Her heart raced faster than when Gareth spooked her on the bike. Her smartwatch indicated her heart rate surpassed a hundred and forty beats per minute and showed no signs of slowing.

Melissa threw open her closet doors. The garment bag protecting her dress hung on the rail. Her hands shook as she reached for the zipper, then slowly pulled down the tab. The gown and coat were as pristine as the day she picked them up from the wedding shop. Relieved it was not ruined, she took some deep cleansing breaths, but they didn't help slow her pulse. Leaving the confines of her room was useless, too, same with splashing cold water on her face and placing a cool cloth on the back of her neck.

Phone snatched off the island, Melissa dropped on the end of the sofa. Danielle hadn't responded to her text about Iain's death. It was the last message in the string, so she typed another one.

I think I'm losing my mind. Help me, please.

She drummed her fingers on her thigh while she waited for a reply.

Sorry didn't respond earlier. Battery was dead. Who's died? Gareth?

A short reply confirmed Gareth was alive. Mel tapped out another message about her nightmare, which took a long time to do. Between her eyes being blurred by tears and trembling, she had to delete and start over repeatedly. Soon after she hit send, her phone rang again. This time it was the ringtone for an incoming call, not a text. She was tempted to let it go to voicemail, but she answered when Danielle's name displayed.

"I am sorry about Iain. Are you all right?"

"Thanks. I don't know. I think so." Melissa pressed her fingertips on her forehead and rubbed as she spoke.

"You shouldn't be alone. Do you want me to come and stay with you?"

Melissa stood, wrapped one arm around her middle and paced. "No. I'd rather be by myself. I need to wrap my head around it."

"Did you tell Gareth?"

"Yes, and I didn't get the reaction I needed or expected.

Gareth acted like a total jerk and said it was karma — that Iain got what he deserved."

"Oh."

"Nobody deserves to be killed," Melissa said, her voice louder than she intended. Danielle had not been the one who'd been unsympathetic and uncaring. "Sorry."

"Don't be. You're grieving. Besides, you and Iain go way back. Gareth might not be pleased, but you have a history with Iain. Gareth's only seen the bad side of him."

"Yeah, I know." Mel sat down on the sofa, tucked her feet under her and pulled the sherpa blanket down from the back. Cocooned in its warmth and weight, she calmed.

"Your dream sounds terrifying — wedding party and guests turning into mannequins? I wouldn't want to be alone after a nightmare like that. Are you sure you don't want me to come?"

"I'll be okay." Buddy scampered up the ramp to the couch and burrowed under the cover. She was not on her own. As long as she had her dog with her, she'd be fine.

"What exactly happened to Iain, or don't you know?"

"The policeman who took me to the hospital said Iain was on his way to work, and he ran the barriers at the level crossing on Bayside Drive."

"Why?"

That was a fair question. "Investigation isn't complete yet, but the police think Iain might have been running late, had his music on too loud and didn't see or hear the train."

"What are the arrangements?"

"Cremation and no visitation." Melissa grabbed a tissue and blew her nose. "Danny, he's left everything to me. The police still have his phone. I need it. When Paul brought me home, I deleted all the pictures I had of him and me from mine. Now I want them back. Or at least the ones on his." The tears flowed again. "His boss, who's a kindly man, came to the condo and is helping me sort through the paperwork. What hurts, even more, the woman he was sleeping with is his boss's wife. It wasn't until the warden and his missus landed in at the hospital that I put the pieces together."

"Oh, sweetie, I wish I was with you so I could give you a hug. I hope Gareth realizes he's been an idiot and apologizes."

"He's already sent me a text. He called me, too. I believe he left a voicemail. I've not replied to either. Letting him stew in his own juices for a while."

Danielle laughed. "It'll look good on him. I should let you get back to whatever you were doing, besides your nightmare. Fresh air will do you the world. Go for a walk, or just sit on your front step. Just don't stay cooped up in your apartment."

"Thanks. I will." Melissa disconnected their call. The chat with her friend helped.

Twenty

jonathans, Water Street, Saint John, New Brunswick

Melissa hurried to the elevator carrying an armload of file folders. "Cheers," she said, panting from the exertion. "Are you new here? I've not seen you before." She brushed her hair out of her face with her upper arm while still holding the bundle of papers.

"I'm not new. I work for *Thacker, Price & Associates* and am here doing an appraisal for the head of *jonathans*. He hired the firm I work for to do a consult on the operations of all the outlets."

Melissa's heart dropped, and her stomach lurched. This store couldn't close. She loved her job, and if that happened, it meant going back home to Ottawa, tail between her legs and admitting defeat to her mother, who was against her moving so far away.

"Nothing to worry about. This location is getting a favourable rating. I love the 'old-fashioned' ambience here, so it would be a shame to alter things. Sometimes, running a successful business is more than stainless steel, plate glass and computerized tills. "By the way, I'm Serenity."

"Melissa Scott." She shook the woman's hand.

Later, Melissa turned up in Serenity's doorway. "I wondered if you fancied a bit of lunch or at least a coffee. The place across the street does amazing food."

A blizzard had blown in off the Bay of Fundy. The small pellets, propelled by the strong wind, pricked and stung Melissa's face like thousands of sharp needles. Days like this were the worst. Unfortunately, throughout the winter, many a nor'easter ravaged the city.

The women advanced into the warmth of the pub. In one of the rooms, a wood fire crackled in a gigantic fireplace. "Let's sit in there," Melissa suggested and asked the hostess if that's where they could be seated.

The heat emanating from the room warmed her, and they had yet to gain entry into the cozy space with the vaulted stone ceiling.

They stood in awkward silence while they waited for someone to seat them. The two seemed like complete strangers, although the women chatted like long-lost friends at the office earlier.

Soon the young woman escorted them to a table and placed menus in front of them.

"Do you come here often?"

"A couple of times a month. Sometimes more." Melissa flipped through the food menu.

"You'll have to guide me."

"What do you like?"

A boyish-looking girl in a t-shirt emblazoned with the name of the pub, jeans and a carpenters apron tied around her waist appeared at the table. "Can I get you something to drink to start?"

"Yes," said Serenity and ordered a dark roast. "One bill, please." She told the waitress and turned to her luncheon partner. "This is on me."

"But …"

"No arguments."

Melissa asked for a Coke and smiled.

"So what do you recommend?"

"Well, the fajitas are to die for. So are the nachos. They do a delicious chicken burger with a boneless, skinless breast, strips of bacon, red onion, lettuce and mayo with a choice of sides if you're not into Mexican. It's one of my favourites."

"Sold."

A few minutes later, the girl placed their beverages in front of them. "You ladies ready?"

"Yes." She nodded to Melissa, indicating she should go first.

After the waitress took her companion's order, Serenity ordered the poultry bun with sweet potato fries for herself.

Over their drinks, they chatted.

"I said earlier I was giving your store a favourable rating. Don't mention any of this to your colleagues. My plan is to centralize all the accounting functions under one roof at the head office in Québec City. People will be given the opportunity to transfer and continue their jobs there if my idea flies. It makes sense rather than having tasks duplicated in various branches."

Melissa swallowed hard. 2017 hadn't been kind to her, and if her job was to disappear, she didn't know if she could rally from that.

"Tell me a bit about yourself."

"I'm originally from Ottawa. Youngest of five with three brothers and a sister."

"Do you see them often?"

"I wish. The closest is my brother, Roger. He lives in Québec City. Christopher is in Alberta, Michael's in England. Amy is in Sudbury."

"A brother in Québec City," Serenity mused. "You would have family nearby if you took the transfer. Any other ties to Saint John?"

"I did." Certainly, the woman seated across the table from her didn't want to hear about Melissa's terrible year. Just the thought of it made her eyes weepy with tears.

"Are you okay?"

"I'll be fine."

"You sure?" Serenity sipped her coffee. "I can be a good listener."

This was the opportunity Melissa needed to unload the burden of events and emotions that tied her in knots.

"My fiancé and I broke up at the end of May. Actually, I dumped him after I caught him cheating. I went to my girlfriend's guesthouse in Percé to escape from the city and the memories. I met a super guy while I was there. A soldier, but he came with a lot of baggage." Melissa gulped down a mouthful of Coke.

"Still, I thought maybe he was the one, but rebound relationships never work. Then in the fall, Iain, my ex-fiancé, was in a horrible car accident and died. After that, my holiday romance with the soldier ended. He couldn't understand my feelings about my ex's death." When she finished, Melissa took a tissue out of her purse and blew her nose.

"I think you'd be a perfect candidate for a position in Québec City. I'll back your request for the transfer, whether my entire idea gets off the ground or not."

That was the best news Melissa had in ages. Escaping Saint John with its unhappy memories. "You've heard my sad tale. What about you?"

"I have no one. No siblings." A lie, but to Serenity, her brother was dead. No parents. "To be honest, I like it that way." If Melissa only knew the truth. Clothes from the Salvation Army. Being razzed at school by the other students because of her outdated apparel. Money was tight most of the time, but when her drug-addict sibling, Erik, stole the meagre amount left in the house, she went hungry many days. His pulling up stakes when he did was the best thing that happened to the family.

"Really? I find that hard to believe." Melissa slowly drank her Coke. "Probably times, my mother wished she didn't have five of us, especially around Easter, Thanksgiving, and the festive season. Add in the out-of-town cousins, and we had at least ten kids running around."

Serenity cringed at the thought. Holidays were never important to her. Time off work was about all they meant. Even then, she worked from home. When she was a young girl, her parents didn't go all gooey over Christmas and Santa Claus, or Easter and the bunny. Valentine's Day didn't mean anything to them. Well, perhaps, because it was the only day of the year they didn't fight. She picked up her mug and drank.

The arrival of their food rescued her from having to answer any more of Melissa's questions. For now.

"I'm headed to Québec City in a couple of weeks after a visit to the Montreal location first. My French is atrocious, so I saved that one for the end. I'll spend my fortnight there, then follow with the week of meetings which my employer and all the store managers will attend."

"You're busy. I suppose being that way keeps you from getting lonely."

"Are you going home for Christmas?"

"No. Not sure if I'll see any of my family this year."

In the short time she spent with the *jonathans* employee, Serenity could tell the idea of not seeing any of her relatives made her sad. "A financial thing? I'll gladly help you out if that's the case."

"Oh, no. Not at all. Even if it were, I couldn't accept it."

"If you decide otherwise, let me know."

Their break ended, and the women returned to the store.

Melissa went about her afternoon routine, but she couldn't stop thinking about Serenity. No relatives. No one to spend time with over the holidays. There was more to her than she shared. Still, trying to pry the secret family lore from her didn't seem right. As it was, she was embarrassed she'd said as much as she did about her life.

Once the audit was completed, in the grand scheme of things, hers and Serenity's paths would never cross again. She wouldn't accept an invitation, either. The woman was too proud. Same with her. She couldn't take her offer of money to help her see her mother and siblings.

Her childhood home in Ottawa was no longer the same now without her brothers and sisters. The last time they were all together as a family was at their father's funeral a year and a half ago. He succumbed to mesothelioma after years of asbestos exposure. Before that, the unexpected death of Roger's wife.

Twenty-One

Roger's Home, Rue des Remparts, Québec City

"Whoa down, sport. Maybe your grandmother would like to watch you unwrap your present. Mom, Mel, come in here. Adam's dying to open his gift from Serenity."

Did he mean Melissa — the girl she met in Saint John? The two had the same surname, so it wasn't inconceivable but improbable. One unexpected guest took her by surprise. But two? Average families did come together on holidays and other occasions. Who else was here?

His sister came into the front room, wiping her hands with a tea towel. "It's wonderful to see you again. I won't hug you. My hands are greasy. Oh, I love your sweater."

Mrs. Scott came in and sat in the armchair near the hearth. Only then did Serenity realize a crackling fire was lit. No wonder the room was so warm.

"Is this the one?" Adam hoisted the enormous package and shook it, rattling the contents.

She squatted beside him. "Yes. Now, if this one is already in your collection, you can exchange it for something different."

The festively coloured wrapping flew into the air and

drifted to the floor. "Wow. Thanks. Not this one. Look, Dad. Ultimate Banking! Can we play now?"

"Later. After the bird is in the oven."

"Aw." Adam's chin sank against his chest.

"Tell you what, why don't you read the rules and figure out how the game goes so when we do sit down, you can teach us?" Serenity said, hoping to cheer up the lad who appeared ready to cry.

The young boy let out a whoop of excitement and tore through the plastic surrounding the box.

Roger's mother and sister started for the kitchen.

"Can I help?" she offered.

"You're fine for now, dear. But later," the family matriarch said.

The words he longed to hear all afternoon rang out. "The turkey is done to perfection," his mother announced.

Not much longer now, and they would all be gathered in the dining room tucking into his mother's famous Christmas dinner.

The women went to help Mrs. Scott, with Roger's dog, Tori, and Buddy in pursuit, leaving Roger and Adam on their own in the living room. The young boy, on his knees in front of the cabinet, meant only one thing. He was looking for another movie.

"Why don't you take a break for now." He tried to make the suggestion gentle. "Lay the table or something."

After the boy trudged off, Roger tipped his head back and closed his eyes. Today was the best Christmas in many years. He dozed off thinking about the day, letting the cooking aromas channel him back to his childhood.

"Supper's ready," his mother said in his ear, jolting him awake.

How long had he napped? His watch displayed he spent well over an hour in the land of nod. Once upright, Roger stretched and ambled to the dining room table. The roasted bird lay on a platter with the carving knife and fork facing his place setting. The women entered from the kitchen with bowls of stuffing, mashed potatoes, turnips and an enormous boat filled with gravy.

Adam scrambled into his chair on Roger's left. Mel and Serenity sat on his right, the latter closest to him, and his mother at the opposite end. Red and green Christmas crackers lay across everyone's plate.

"Can we pull them now, Dad?"

"Yes."

The young boy plucked his from both ends, and with a yank, twist, and a pop, pulled the paper tube apart. The others were more subdued when they opened theirs. His mother and sister got hold of the strip inside and tugged. A loud snap echoed, but they still had to open the cylinder.

Tori and her companion, Buddy, bolted from the room at the unexpected noise.

Serenity struggled, and Roger reached over and opened it for her, then attended to his own. A shiny gold foil crown and riddle were the only consistent items. Each cracker held a unique gift. Adam got a deck of miniature playing cards; Melissa got a silver-tone pen; his mother, pierced earrings; Serenity a corkscrew in the shape of a wine bottle. His trinket was a luggage tag.

"You're the man of the house, Roger. Carving the turkey goes with the title," Mrs. Scott said.

"No pressure, bro'." Melissa smiled and giggled.

He cooked whole chickens and cut them up, but it was just him and Adam on those occasions. Even when Brigitte was alive, he butchered the poor beast in the kitchen, not under three women's scrutiny.

Roger stood and picked up the carving utensils. "I make no promises." He stabbed the fork through the golden brown crispy skin into the breast.

"I want the pope's nose, Dad, and a drumstick."

He removed the requested parts from the bird and deposited them on Adam's plate. No need for formalities with him. With the leg off, the enormous turkey was easier for him to carve. Once sliced, he placed the pieces on another platter.

Potatoes, turnip and dressing, and the fowl serving dish passed from one person to the next round the table, followed by the gravy and cranberries.

For the first few minutes, no one spoke. They were busy savouring the feast in front of them.

"What a delicious dinner."

"Thank you, dear. So what do you do for a living?"

"I'm a business consultant working for a firm in Toronto. I just completed a study for *jonathans* and hosted a week of meetings going over the results."

"I met Serenity in Saint John," said Melissa.

Mrs. Scott nodded.

"Small world, eh, mom?" Roger shoved a forkful of turkey and stuffing into his mouth.

"Dad, can Serenity come live with us?"

The statement made Roger choke and forced him to take a mouthful of water. She turned crimson with embarrassment. At least he assumed it was the reason for her blush. He was fond of the woman — exceptionally fond — but it was far too soon to even think of living with her.

An awkward silence fell over the room. The only sounds were cutlery against china. Then the pitch changed to on glass. Melissa was standing tapping her goblet with the back edge of the knife blade. "I have an announcement to make."

"Don't keep us in suspense, sis."

"I'm moving to Québec City."

"Wow, Auntie Mel!"

"What brought this on?" asked Roger.

"Gareth and I split up." She choked back a sob.

Apparently, this fellow, whoever he was, was special to her. "You never referred to him in any of your emails. I'm sorry about you and Iain breaking up. Ma told me."

Melissa fled from the room in tears.

Mrs. Scott gave him the evil eye.

"What did I do wrong?" he asked.

"Your sister has had a horrible year. Gareth is the man she became acquainted with. When Iain was killed in a car accident, she and Gareth split up."

No wonder Mel was so upset. Roger found his sister crying in the kitchen. "I'm sorry." Melissa buried her face in his chest and cried. He drew her into a hug. She was his baby sister, and it grieved him to see her this way. "Ma only told me you and Iain broke up — no details. I'd like to know what happened, but in your own time and not before."

"Thanks. 2017 hasn't been one of my finer years."

"You ready to go back and eat?"

Melissa nodded. Roger wrapped his arm around her shoulders and walked her back to the dining room.

Once seated, she carried on, "I'm leaving Saint John. I have nothing to keep me there now. I'm having my things shipped here to this address. Hope you don't mind." Melissa stopped talking long enough to swallow some water, then continued. "Serenity wants to move all the accounting functions here to Québec City. She helped me wangle a transfer to the *jonathans* store here. Isn't that brilliant? Don't worry; I won't be under your feet for too long. I'm looking for an apartment, so once I find one, I'll be out of your hair."

The final disclosure stunned Roger.

Melissa smiled at him.

During the silence, Serenity stood. "Since this is a day of announcements, I'm going to make one, too."

Now what? Roger took in a lungful of air and grinned at her despite worrying about what her revelation might be.

"After the last meeting Friday afternoon, my boss came to me and told me I got the promotion I wanted so badly for so long. So corner office, a personal assistant, and dare I say, a substantial pay raise. After being here and experiencing a proper Christmas …"

"I don't know how …," said Roger.

"A lot more than I ever had. Anyway, today and this last week spending time with you, your family, and your wacky dog showed me there's more to life than a job and money."

Puzzled, he tried to work out where she was going with this statement. He didn't have long to wait.

"Jonathan Drake has offered me an upper management position. He wants me to stay on and see this project through to completion. After that, I'll be doing what I did through *Thacker, Price & Associates* but dedicated to just one firm — *jonathans*."

Melissa squealed. "That's wonderful. We'll be working together all of the time."

Serenity's news pleased him, too. If she moved to Québec City or the vicinity, he would be able to see her.

"I didn't say yes, yet. I told Mr. Drake I needed to think about it."

"'tis a big decision."

Serenity nodded and sat.

"You know how Serenity and I met, so how did you meet her, Rog?"

"Tori knocked her down," said Adam, who then immediately changed the subject. "What's for dessert, Grandma?"

"We'd had her out for a walk off-leash over at the Plains of Abraham and just stepped onto Dufferin Terrace. Tori took off, and when she was about ten feet away from Serenity launched into the air. I'd never seen my dog move so fast."

"I'm surprised you weren't hurt," Mrs. Scott said.

"Makes two of us," Roger said. "So there you go, Mel. That's how I met Serenity."

"Grandma, dessert," Adam whined.

"Oh yes, pumpkin pie, fruit cake, shortbread and plum pudding."

"Can I have a piece of everything?"

"Adam." Roger's tone spoke volumes, and he didn't need to say another word.

"Pie, please."

"Finish what's on your plate first."

Dishes carried through to the kitchen, and remnants scraped into the garbage, Mrs. Scott arranged the fine china plates and cutlery in the dishwasher.

A fresh pot of dark roast waited on the coffeemaker. Roger took the carafe through to the dining room.

After their dessert and the table cleared, Adam brought out Monopoly Ultimate Banking. Roger sat back and played spectator, allowing his mother to take part.

Many hours later, they declared the tournament over and crowned Serenity the winner.

Twenty-Two

Roger's Home, Rue des Remparts, Québec City

Melissa walked into the living room with a steaming mug of hot chocolate in each hand. The kitchen door swung on its hinges in her wake.

Roger sat on the chaise portion of the sectional, aiming the remote control at the television — the image continually changing. He didn't acknowledge her even when she stepped in front of him and placed the hot cup of cocoa on the coffee table.

"We're a right pair. Sitting home on New Year's Eve," said Melissa.

"Single father life. I'm used to staying in at night. You can go out if you want."

"What, and leave you here moping on your own? Not a chance."

Roger shifted on the sofa, so he was facing his sister. "How did you and this Gareth guy meet? Ma never told me."

"That's because she doesn't know."

"What do you mean, she doesn't know?"

"I didn't tell her, and if I tell you, you must swear you won't." A cold sweat formed on the nape of Melissa's neck.

Surely, she could trust her brother to keep her secret.

"I won't tell."

She sipped her cocoa. "Hey, this stuff is yummy. Where from?"

"La Fudgerie in Lower Town. Now tell me how you two met."

"Buddy and I walked out to Percé Rock. I wasn't paying attention to the time or the weather, and he was terrorizing the gannets that nest there. Anyway, we were stranded by the storm and the incoming tide. Gareth persuaded a whale-watching boat pilot to take him out to rescue us."

"I can understand why you don't want ma to find out."

Seated on the opposite end of the couch, she curled one leg underneath the other one. "So why aren't you and Serenity doing something tonight? I'm here, so Adam's not alone." She leaned closer to her brother.

"She's not into holidays. Planned on a quiet night in."

"She enjoyed herself with us at Christmas if you ask me."

"Yes, she did."

"Then phone her," Melissa exclaimed.

Tori lifted her head from her bed. Roger turned and glared at her.

"Oops. Sorry." She giggled. "If you don't call Serenity. I will."

"At ten-thirty at night. No."

"Then walk up there and quit being such a misery gut."

A knock on the front door followed by Tori's barking interrupted their banter. Roger rose from the sectional before the dog barked the house down. "Shush," he commanded. The black Labrador retriever stopped instantly but hovered next to him.

Being on her own for a moment allowed Melissa to take custody of the remote control. She hit the guide button and searched the directory for something to watch. Her brother's choice of programs left much to be desired if he kept it on a single channel long enough.

"Someone for you," he said.

"Hi, Mel. I missed you."

She spun around. "G-Gareth. What are you doing here?"

"I came to see you. Try to atone for being a total idiot."

"Well, you two have some catching up to do. Maybe I will go meet up with Serenity."

"How did you find me?" Melissa stood her ground by the end of the sofa.

"You said you had a brother in Québec City when we first met. Valcartier isn't all that far away. Had plenty of time to think back on what a jerk I was and even more to track down your sibling. I took a chance with it being the holidays; you'd be here."

"Whatever you two do, don't let Tori out. She hates fireworks," Roger said before he shut the front door behind him.

"Rog and I were having hot chocolate. Do you want one?"

"Sure." Gareth bent down and removed his snow-covered boots.

"You can hang your coat on the hook in the hall," she said and disappeared around the corner into the kitchen.

Gareth was the last person on earth she expected to find in her brother's living room on New Year's Eve. His harsh words about Iain had hurt her, and she lashed out back at him.

When she pushed through the door with the mug of cocoa for Gareth, his presence on the other side startled her, and she jumped. Hot liquid slopped over the rim and covered her hand. She quickly put the cup on the counter and ran her hand under cold water.

In a flash, he was behind her with his arms around her waist.

"I'm sorry," he whispered.

She leaned back into him and turned her head, so her cheek rested against his collarbone. "Sorry about this? Sorry about the things you said about Iain?"

"Everything. Can we go into the other room and sit down?"

"Sure."

Gareth picked up the drink Melissa made him and held the kitchen door open for her. She followed him back into the living room and plopped down on the end of the couch she occupied earlier in the evening. He remained standing.

"You not going to take your coat off?"

"Depends on the reaction I get once I say everything I came to say."

Finally, Gareth sat. He took her hands in his and brought them to his mouth and kissed each one. The red marks where the hot chocolate slopped over the mug, thanks to him, received extra attention.

"When Iain died, I was in a bad place. My meds weren't working anymore. The doctors were trying others and experimenting with dosages, but nothing helped. At one point, I spent some time in a mental ward. I'd heard your voice inside the walls and tried to tear them apart to rescue you." He wrung his hands and bowed his head in shame.

"On top of that, they just posted me to the transition centre, which had me more depressed than usual. I know you had a past with Iain, and I don't want to take that away from you. Never wanted to do that. I love you, Mel. Have since I pulled you out of the water at Percé Rock."

Her head was bowed, and he lifted her chin. Her eyes were glassy with tears. Gareth leaned closer to her and kissed her eyelids. "After I put both my size twelves in my mouth at the same instant, it was too late. I blew it. Your reaction at the time proved it, and you not contacting me afterwards punctuated it."

A tear dripped down her cheek, and he dashed it away with his thumb. "What's kept me going is looking at the pictures you put on my phone of us at Percé."

"Kept you going?" she asked.

"I still think of suicide. Wouldn't be the first soldier to kill myself thanks to PTSD."

Buddy emerged from under the Christmas tree and approached Gareth, who patted the couch and invited the dachshund to join him.

"Roger doesn't like the dogs on the furniture."

"Well, then I'll make sure he stays on my lap." He petted the pooch and cuddled him under his arm. "Okay, Bud, I'm going to need your help here. I'm trying to apologize for being an idiot, and I don't think your human is taking heed."

A soft giggle reached his ears. Gareth turned his attention away from Melissa's dog and saw a smile on her face. So far, he had dominated the conversation, not giving Melissa a chance to speak, save for a few short words mainly unrelated to the topic.

"You were in a bad place? How do you think I felt getting calls from the police on Iain's phone? I thought it was him harassing me again until the cop got a word in telling me not to hang up. I found out then Iain named me as his next of kin. But the kicker was, Iain's boss and wife showed up at the hospital. What do you think it was like seeing madam home wrecker sitting across the corridor from me with a face on her like a smacked bum?"

"Oh, Mel, if I only knew." Gareth pulled her close and kissed the top of her head. "We were both in dark places. Still doesn't excuse the things I said about Iain." He kept his arms around her, and they sat in silence. Selfish or not, he needed to turn the discussion back in the right direction.

"One of my medics proposed an emotional support dog — a service dog for veterans and other folks who suffer from PTSD. Don't suppose you know anyone like that? Been working with one for a while now — a golden retriever. He senses when I'm about to have a meltdown and is at my side to prevent it from happening."

Except for the one severe episode in Percé, Melissa was his crutch. He didn't dare say that out loud because she would take it the wrong way and think he was calling her a dog. Instead, he pulled out his smartphone and scrolled through the photos.

Gareth handed the device to her. "This is Percival. He's my ESD. I call him Percy because it reminds me of where you and I met."

"He's beautiful. I love his name. And you named him after

the village. Sweet. Where is he? Did you bring him with you?"

"No. Left him back at the base. You'll meet him soon enough. After I got Percy, I took him with me, and we went home to Saint-Hyacinthe. I wouldn't have had the courage to do that before him. It was the first time I went to my parents' house since returning from Afghanistan. I spoke with Normand's parents, too. I was so sure they blamed me for what happened to him, but they didn't."

With both hands free, Gareth was able to dig a cube-shaped object out of his leather jacket's inside pocket. He positioned himself in front of Melissa. "Miss Scott. Could I draw your attention away from the dog photos to the small box I'm holding in my hand?"

She turned to him. The Christmas tree lights reflected in her beautiful brown eyes. He shifted his position so he was on one knee.

"Melissa, I know I've been an idiot, but I love you. I want to spend the rest of my life with you. Will you do me the honour of becoming my wife?"

Her hands shot up to her face and covered her mouth. Gareth opened the box. "Will you marry me, Mel?"

"Yes," Melissa shrieked. "Of course, I will!"

She said yes. Gareth exhaled the breath he held since he asked the question. He wrapped his arms around her waist and hugged her. The gesture pulled her off the couch, and they fell to the floor in fits of laughter, which got Tori and Buddy barking.

"Quiet, you two," she scolded. "You'll wake Adam."

"What's going on downstairs, Auntie Mel?" the young boy hollered.

"I just got engaged. Come down and meet my fiancé."

Melissa pulled herself to her feet, smoothed down the front of her clothes, and stole glances at the diamond solitaire ring set in white gold. The facets caught the Christmas tree lights and sparkled in the same colours. Gareth raised himself off the area rug and joined her.

Footfalls thundered down the stairs. For a small boy, he was loud. In no time, he stood in the living room, both dogs vying for his attention.

"Adam, this is Gareth."

"Hi," the boy said quietly.

"And Gareth, this is my nephew, Adam."

"Hey, kiddo. You look like your father."

"You know my dad?" he asked, his eyes wide.

"Not really. Met the man tonight when I came to speak to your aunt."

The little boy crept closer to the couple.

"Don't be afraid, Adam. Gareth won't hurt you. Adam here is quite the board game fanatic."

"Really. I wonder where he got that from? Any ideas, Mel?"

She smiled. "Serenity, my brother's friend. He went to visit her when you arrived. Anyway, she bought Adam the new version of Monopoly — Ultimate Banking — for Christmas. Needless to say, we played all evening."

"Can we play now, Auntie Mel?"

"It's late. You should be getting back to your bed."

"Can I at least stay up until midnight?"

"All right."

"Yay," he shouted and leapt over the back of the sofa.

"Does your brother have any mistletoe in this house?" Gareth asked.

"No, why?"

"We'll just have to pretend we're standing under it now," he said and brushed his lips against hers.

Intense, passionate and electrifying. Melissa's knees weakened. The power behind his kiss came unexpectedly but certainly not unwelcome.

"Ew, get a room, will you?"

The moment was broken by her nephew's comment.

New Year's celebrations started on the television. In the distance, the fireworks banged and crackled. Tori darted upstairs.

"We had a deal, young man. Midnight and then to bed."

"All right," he said and headed towards the stairs, his chin on his chest. At the foot of the staircase, Adam paused. "Can you guys tuck me in? That way, Gareth can see my room."

"That's another thing. Everyone has to look at Adam's room the first time they visit."

"Must be quite the place, is it?"

Melissa followed Adam upstairs, and Gareth walked behind her.

Adam opened his bedroom door. "Come on," he urged and advanced into the darkened zone.

Once Gareth reached it, he turned on the light. All things solar system decorated the interior. A mural of the cosmos covered two adjoining walls. The others were painted dark blue. A mobile of the planets hung suspended over the head of the bed. Even the bedding matched the space theme.

"Very nice. You're into astronomy, I see."

"Yes. One day I'm going to be an astronaut and go to the International Space Station." His enthusiasm gushed.

"Good for you. I think you might just do it, or whatever comes after the space station. Did your aunt tell you that one night after we met in Percé, we went stargazing?"

"No."

Melissa lifted the covers and nodded to her nephew that it was time to go back to bed. "I don't want your father giving me a hard time because I let you get up and see in the New Year."

"K."

"I'll tell you about our night under the stars another time."

Adam tucked in; she motioned to Gareth to leave the room. They returned to the living room and snuggled together on the couch.

This night was perfect. The man she loved with all her being was here with her. He'd asked her to marry him. Best of all, she said, 'yes.'

Twenty-Three

Melissa's apartment, Coburg Street, Saint John

Instead of marrying Iain on New Year's Day, Melissa left Buddy with Roger and Adam and boarded a train to Moncton followed by a bus to Saint John. She carried her purse, phone and charging cable, and keys to her apartment, which needed to be packed up, so everything was boxed and ready when the movers arrived. The first day of work at the *jonathans* head office was the following Monday — January 8.

When she finally got home, the moving company had left a dozen flat-pack boxes in the downstairs hallway for her. She retrieved the flat sheets of cardboard and dragged them up to the top floor. After work the next day, she would borrow a roll of tape and machine from the store's packing department.

The day after her wedding ceremony nightmare, she called the bridal boutique to ask if she could return the garment because she'd never use it. The shop manager refused, so it meant one more thing to drag with her when she returned to Québec City.

Melissa purchased the gown for a winter wedding. She and Gareth never set a date when he proposed, but the idea of wearing a dress when she married him that was bought for another didn't sit well with her.

Thanks to Mr. Carruthers' help, Iain's estate was settled quickly, and a healthy nest egg sat in her bank account. She sold the Water Street condo, furnished, at a profit. But with the mortgage insurance, even a dollar was profit. The only items she removed from there were personal effects that would be of no interest to anyone. The warden took back the uniforms; the other clothing went to charity.

The police returned Iain's phone not long before she left for her brother's. It still languished in the evidence bag on the island. The pictures were the only things in which she had any interest. Her's and Iain's adventures together. She had been stupid to delete them from her iPhone.

Melissa's return to work after the Christmas holidays was bittersweet. It was her last week in the New Brunswick store. Come Friday, she would leave to start her new life in Québec City with a new job in the head office of *jonathans*. Family and fiancé and soon her friend Serenity would all be reunited.

She didn't tell Gareth her news. How did she manage to forget? Giddy with excitement over his proposal played a huge factor. She grabbed her phone and tapped out a text message.

Call me when you get a chance. Got something to tell you. I forgot New Year's Eve.

She hit send and returned her phone to her blazer pocket. About half an hour later, her jacket vibrated. Melissa got up from her desk and walked into the corridor. Gareth's name filled the display. She swiped the screen and answered the call. "Hi, Gareth."

"Hi. What's up?"

"I can't believe I didn't tell you that starting next Monday I'm going to be working at the *jonathans* store in Québec City. Roger's friend, my friend, too, Serenity, arranged my transfer. I don't know how far the base is from there, but it's got to be a lot closer than Saint John," she babbled.

"I can understand how a minor detail like that could slip your mind," he teased. "I asked you to marry me that night."

"I'm serious." Melissa put her other hand over her left ear to make it easier to hear Gareth and leaned back. "I have nothing to tie me to the city anymore, so the timing was perfect."

"That's fantastic news. It really is. I think it took me about forty-five minutes New Year's Eve to go from the base to your brother's, what with the road closures for the holiday events. Normally, about half an hour. I guess you'll try to find a place in that area? I can't imagine your brother wanting a permanent house guest."

"I wouldn't want to live with him full time either," she laughed. "We had enough of each other, growing up in Ottawa."

"I better let you get back to work. I'll see you some time next week." Gareth disconnected the call.

Melissa tipped her head back. Maybe 2018 would be the year she got her life on the right track.

Epilogue

Fortin's Guesthouse, Percé, Québec

June 2018 ...

Mrs. Scott came down from Ottawa to Québec City by train on Sunday, June 3. Melissa and Gareth, and their entourage, walked from her new home near the Hotel Clarendon to her brother's. Except for the extra dog and one more person, it was like Christmas again. Buddy and Tori had met back then and gotten along. Percy, the laid-back goofball that he was, mixed well with everyone.

The following day, Gareth picked Melissa up at her apartment. She was ready and waiting when he arrived.

"Isn't it bad luck to see the bride before the big day?" he asked.

"I don't think it counts if it's two days before," she said and kissed him on the cheek.

Melissa wheeled a hardshell suitcase out the front door and handed it off to Gareth, who stowed it in the back of his Jeep. Next came the garment bag with her wedding gown. She refused to let him even handle it and found a place where she could hang it in the back. Percy snoozed on the backseat throughout the loading until Melissa set Buddy's carrier on the floor in the rear footwell.

"He doesn't need to ride in that. He can sit up there with his friend."

Crate opened, she lifted the dachshund out, placed him on the seat with the other dog and closed the door. A Monday departure allowed them Tuesday to rest and relax before the event. With two dogs that needed bathroom breaks and she and Gareth, it could take upwards of ten hours to drive to Danielle's.

The suspension in Gareth's Jeep Wrangler was stiff, which didn't seem to bother him. Military vehicles were designed to be functional, not comfortable, so he was likely used to it. She had only ridden in it a few times and preferred the motorcycle to this. After riding in it all day, she would need a full body massage to remove the knots from her back.

"Think I'll buy a sidecar for the Norton and goggles for Percy, and he can enjoy going out with me."

"You're nuts."

"And that's why you love me. We'll pick up a set for Buddy, too. Maybe leather jackets for the two of them."

Melissa swatted his arm playfully, which brought both dogs to attention at her left elbow.

By the time they reached Percé and Danielle's house, it was going on eight o'clock. The designated parking area was packed. She recognized Paul's BMW and Gilles' truck, surprised it still ran, but none of the other vehicles.

Danielle came outside and wrapped her friend into a warm hug as they unloaded. "I didn't think you would ever arrive. We were starting to worry." She grabbed the garment bag containing her friend's wedding dress and carefully draped it over her arm. "You and your mom are sharing the room you stayed in last summer. All right with you?"

"Sure."

"I gave Gilles and Paul the room with twin beds, put Serenity in one of the doubles, and Amy in the other."

"She's here? I didn't think she was coming. Something about no money and couldn't get the time off."

"We had to have some surprises for you." Danielle walked Melissa into the house, her arm around her shoulders.

Roger, Serenity, Adam and Tori sat in the corner by the fireplace in conversation with an older couple she didn't recognize. Gareth's parents, maybe? She had never met them before. Her sister, Amy, stood near the island with her back to her, chatting with Paul and Gilles.

Speaking of Gareth, he was still outside, unloading her things from the Jeep. She turned and dashed out the door. "Sorry about that," she panted, out of breath from running.

"Just your suitcase, Buddy and his crate left? Nothing else?"

"No. Anything else belongs to you. You coming in?"

Gareth's face paled.

"It'll be fine. I'll be with you. Percy will be beside you and on you." Melissa picked a golden hair off his shirt. "Good thing I know where this came from, and I'm not the jealous type." She smiled at him, and the corners of his mouth twitched and turned into a full-on grin.

"What are we waiting for then?" He extended the handle on her suitcase, leaned into the vehicle and grabbed Percy's lead with the other. While Gareth did that, Melissa tended to Buddy's crate and him. They walked to the house when they had their charges, Gareth trundling Mel's luggage behind him.

The gentleman who had been speaking with her brother and his family earlier strode towards them. "Gareth, my boy. We thought you changed your mind and run off, but if this lovely young lady is the one you were running off with, well done."

Melissa's curiosity as to the man's identity was satisfied.

"Evie, come and meet Gareth's fiancée," he called to his wife across the crowded room.

When she arrived at her husband's side, Gareth made the introductions. "Mom, Dad, this is Melissa. Mel, these are my parents, Kenneth and Evelyn."

"Ken and Evie, please," said Mrs. Young.

"Pleased to meet you," she said and extended her hand. "I see you met my brother, Roger."

"Yes. We must get back to him and his lovely family."

Melissa turned to Gareth. "Well, shall I introduce you to the rest of the crowd?"

He sucked in a deep breath. She switched Percy's lead to his right hand and took his left — his discomfort was palpable. Silently, Mel begged him to hold it together and not break down.

The couple worked their way around the room. Melissa introduced her siblings but depended on them to present their plus ones. "Michael, I'm so glad you got here from England," she gushed and hugged him.

"Chuffed mom contacted me when she did, or I would have been across at New Year's. By the way, sorry to hear about Iain."

"Thanks. Gareth, this is Michael. I'm afraid I don't know your name," she said to the girl on her brother's arm.

"I'm Jennifer. Jennifer Fox."

After chatting briefly with them, they moved on to Christopher and his guest and, in time, made it to the island where Amy stood with Paul and Gilles.

"Who's this handsome boy?" she asked, looking at the golden retriever.

"He's my emotional support dog," he said.

"Gareth served in Afghanistan," Melissa explained but didn't say any more than that. Gareth's hand shook in hers. "Do you want to go outside for some air?"

"Sure."

Mel guided him through the crowded room and out to the verandah.

Gareth gripped the railing, sure a psychotic break was imminent. Percy nudged his hand with his nose. The panic attack continued. The dog got up on its back feet and placed its front paws on Gareth's chest. Slowly, the man calmed and his grip on the handrail loosened.

"Let's sit down," Melissa said.

He dropped into one of the chairs, and his faithful four-legged companion sat at his feet with a paw in his lap. "Good boy, Percy," Gareth said as he petted the dog's head.

This was the first anxiety attack he suffered in ages. Of all places, too. In front of Melissa's family and his parents. How he would survive the ceremony the day after tomorrow was a mystery. They, well, Mel mostly, had planned an outdoor wedding, so that might not be bad. What if it rained? What if it was moved indoors? That thought terrified him. Were any of her siblings aware of his PTSD?

What did they think of a grown man needing an emotional support dog? Melissa mentioned to one of them that he served in Afghanistan, not that he remembered which one. They'd put it together if they added things up.

His mother and father knew of his problems after the war. Gareth had spilled his guts about the nightmares, hallucinations, and guilt over his friend dying in the explosion when he finally visited them and Normand's parents in Saint-Hyacinthe.

In two days, he would marry the girl he fell in love with here in the village of Percé. If not for the leave, granted by the military, to get his act together, he never would have met her.

A soft hand caressed his face, and a pair of concerned eyes gazed into his. Gareth twisted his head and pressed his lips against her palm.

Their moment was interrupted as guests filed out the front door and made their way to the vehicles in which they had arrived. Melissa's siblings all kissed her on the cheek as they passed. Danielle followed and waved everyone off.

Gareth stood. "I best go, too. Glad I arranged a late check-in." He took Mel's hand and helped her to her feet. "Tomorrow is the day it's bad luck for me to see you. Guess we'll have to find something else to do." He kissed her and started for his Jeep with Percy trotting beside him.

After he had the dog in the rear seat, he turned to the verandah where Melissa stood with her friend and said, "Don't be getting yourself into a bind where you'll need rescuing." He grinned, climbed behind the wheel and drove off.

Wednesday, June 6, 2018, exactly a year to the date Melissa and Gareth met, dawned sunny and bright. A soft, salty breeze blew in from over the Gulf of St. Lawrence, and the white paper lanterns on the gazebo swayed in its wake.

The *jonathans* alterations department had done a fantastic job of transforming her wedding gown. The fur from the coat now trimmed the spaghetti straps and the bodice of the dress. The sides had been taken in, giving it shape. The pearl buttons and sequins now adorned that part of the garment. There had even been enough of the original trim left to cover the comb that held her veil in place.

Rows of white, wooden folding chairs, separated by a wide aisle, faced the pavilion. A table covered with a fitted covering served as the altar and where the bride and groom would sign the register.

Two guests had been added to Melissa's list. Their invitation included the instructions that they weren't to tell anyone they were coming. She wanted it to be a surprise for Gareth.

The mid-week date was unusual but memorable to those who knew its significance. Most of the guests didn't.

Family members began to arrive shortly before two that afternoon for the three o'clock ceremony. The location of the gazebo and rows of seats were outside the kitchen window. Christopher and Michael escorted people to their chairs. An officiant had been secured from the village, and he stood in front of the makeshift altar.

The closer the time came, the more nervous Melissa became. Her mother, Danielle and Serenity fussed over her, making sure she was perfect.

Gareth had not arrived yet, or if he had, he managed to sneak by without her seeing.

Christopher entered the house through the back door. "Everyone's here. Are you ready, mom?"

Mrs. Scott kissed her daughter and left with her oldest son via the front door to be escorted to her seat. Serenity squeezed Melissa's hand, and she and the others followed.

Roger met them at the corner of the house. Not long after their father had died, Mel asked him if and when the time came, would he walk her down the aisle.

Soft music reached her ears. Amy, Serenity, and Danielle started down the path to the altar. When she and her brother got to the last row of seats, Gareth stood. He looked so handsome in his full dress uniform. Paul and Gilles were with him, and Percy and Buddy, both dogs wearing black tuxedo bandanas with matching bow ties.

Melissa blinked back tears of joy. She didn't think of including their pets in the wedding, but Gareth had. Her heart melted at the gesture, but where was Tori? Roger brought his black Lab with him. There she was, sitting at Adam's feet, her collar adorned with flowers.

The ceremony went off without incident. After the newlyweds signed the register, congratulatory handshakes and kisses made the rounds.

"You've made me so happy," Melissa whispered.

"Not as much as you made me," Gareth said and kissed her full on the lips again.

"Congratulations, Gareth."

"Madame Courcy. Monsieur Lévesque. What a surprise," he exclaimed, pumping the man's hand in enthusiasm. "How?"

"Your lovely bride invited us."

"Oh, Mel." He enveloped her in a hug. "You don't know how happy this makes me."

A loud shrieking whistle sounded, and a silence fell over the crowd.

"Photo time," Christopher announced.

Pictures with Gareth's parents and Mrs. Scott. More with Normand's. Still more with the Scott clan. The dogs were front and centre in every photograph. The shoot finished with just the bride and groom and Buddy and Percy.

Danielle and Paul joined them. "It looks like your sister and my brother are getting pretty chummy," she said.

They sat next to each other, Gilles twisted in his chair with his arm around the back of hers. They appeared to have hit it off. Back in the day, Amy was snobbish and didn't pay any attention to him. She spent most of her time aspiring to be one of the 'in' kids who came from wealthier families.

"Danny and I have something we'd like to tell you," said Paul.

"We didn't want it to steal the thunder from your day," she added.

"What?"

"There will be another wedding here at Fortin's Guesthouse."

"You and Danielle?"

"Yes." He pulled her close to him and kissed her on the cheek.

"So now I know why all the questions when you drove me back to Saint John last summer."

"We didn't want to do it without your blessing," said Paul.

"Have you set a date?" Melissa asked.

"Not yet. We wanted you to be the first to know, and, of course, you and Gareth will be our witnesses."

Melissa threw her arms around Danielle and squealed. "I'm excited for you." There was a time and not so long ago, she wouldn't have felt that way about her best friend engaged to Paul Sutton, but now she had the man of her dreams as her husband, she was thrilled. There would be another wedding here in Percé. Danielle deserved to be happy, and if Paul was the man who made her so, then good for him.

<<<O>>>

Also by Melanie Robertson-King

A Shadow in the Past (out of print)
4RV Publishing

The Consequences Collection
Tim's Magic Christmas
The Secret of Hillcrest House
A Shadow in the Past (second edition)
Shadows From Her Past
YESTERDAY TODAY ALWAYS
Cole's Notes (Revised version)
It Happened on Dufferin Terrace
All Aboard the Canadian with Buddy and his Four Fantastic
Furry Friends!
It Happened in Gastown
(King Park Press)

Cole's Notes (A Short Story)
EFD1: Starship Goodwords – a cross genre anthology
(CARRICK PUBLISHING, 2012)

Future Titles in the *It Happened* Series ...
featuring the Layne and Scott families

It Happened in Niagara Falls

It Happened at Lake Louise

MELANIE ROBERTSON-KING

https://melanierobertson-king.com

Melanie Robertson-King has always been a fan of the written word. Growing up as an only child, her face was almost always buried in a book from the time she could read. Her father was one of the thousands of Home Children sent to Canada through the auspices of The Orphan Homes of Scotland, and she has been fortunate to be able to visit her father's homeland many times and even met the Princess Royal (Princess Anne) at the orphanage where he was raised.

It Happened at Percé Rock is Melanie's eleventh book.

www.ingramcontent.com/pod-product-compliance
Lightning Source LLC
Chambersburg PA
CBHW020331260626
47156CB00004B/1467